A Crabby [Book]

Party Time, Crabby!

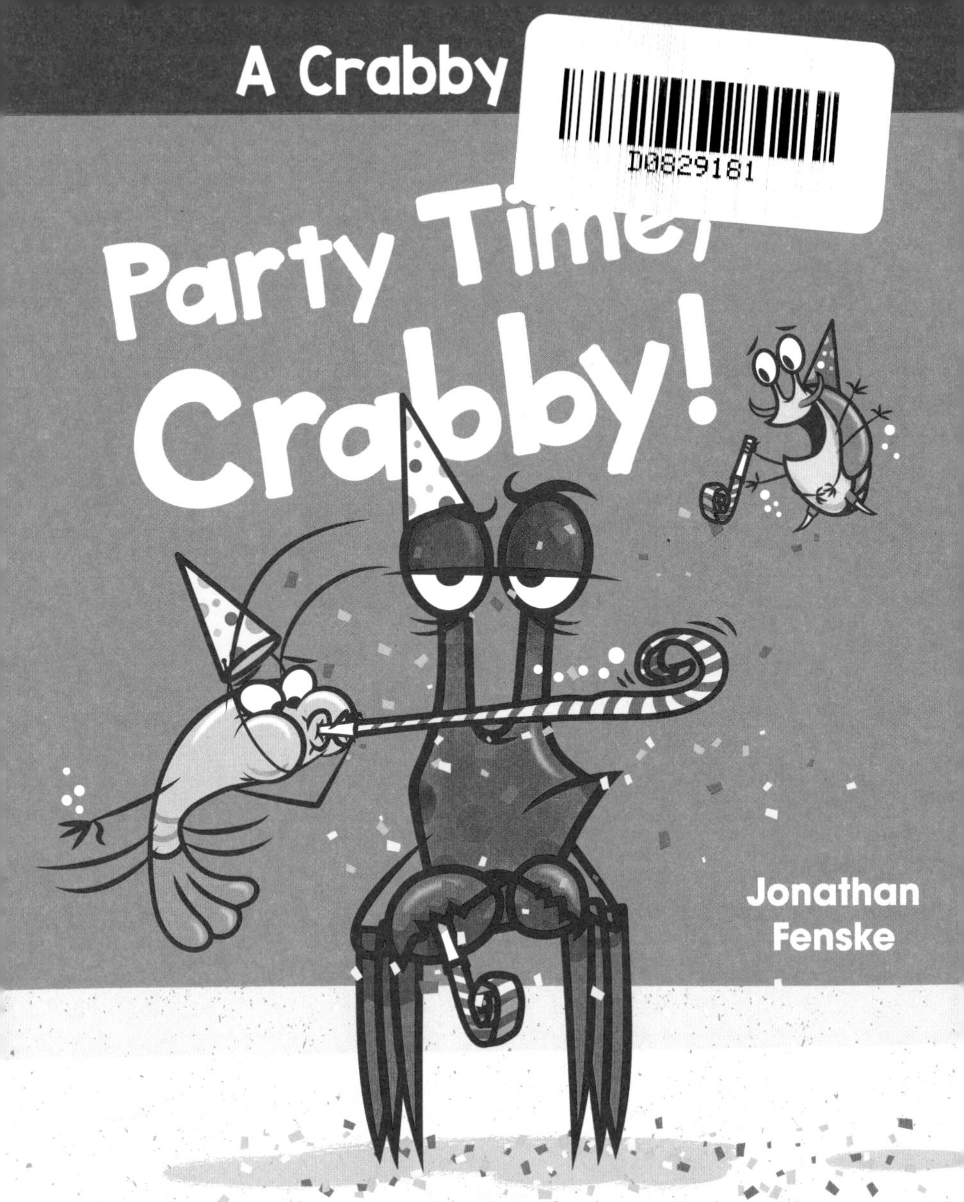

Jonathan Fenske

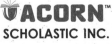

ACORN™
SCHOLASTIC INC.

For all the wallflowers.

Library of Congress Cataloging-in-Publication Data

Names: Fenske, Jonathan, author, illustrator.
Title: Party time, Crabby! / Jonathan Fenske.
Description: First edition. | New York : Acorn/Scholastic, 2023. | Series: A Crabby book ; 6 | Audience: Ages 4–6. | Audience: Grades K–1. | Summary: Crabby is expecting just another boring day in the ocean, but Plankton decides to throw a best friends party—and even Crabby's long list of things he wants at the party will not deter him.
Identifiers: LCCN 2022023059 | ISBN 9781338767940 (paperback) | ISBN 9781338767957 (hardback)
Subjects: LCSH: Crabs—Juvenile fiction. | Plankton—Juvenile fiction. | Parties—Juvenile fiction. | Friendship—Juvenile fiction. | Humorous stories. | CYAC: Crabs—Fiction. | Plankton—Fiction. | Parties—Fiction. | Friendship—Fiction. | Humorous stories. | BISAC: JUVENILE FICTION / Readers / Beginner | JUVENILE FICTION / Animals / Marine Life | LCGFT: Picture books. | Humorous fiction.
Classification: LCC PZ7.F34843 Par 2023 | DDC 813.6 (E)—dc23/eng/20220516

LC record available at https://lccn.loc.gov/2022023059

10 9 8 7 6 5 4 3 2 1   23 24 25 26 27

Printed in China   62
First edition, February 2023
Edited by Katie Heit
Book design by Sarah Dvojack

THE PLAN

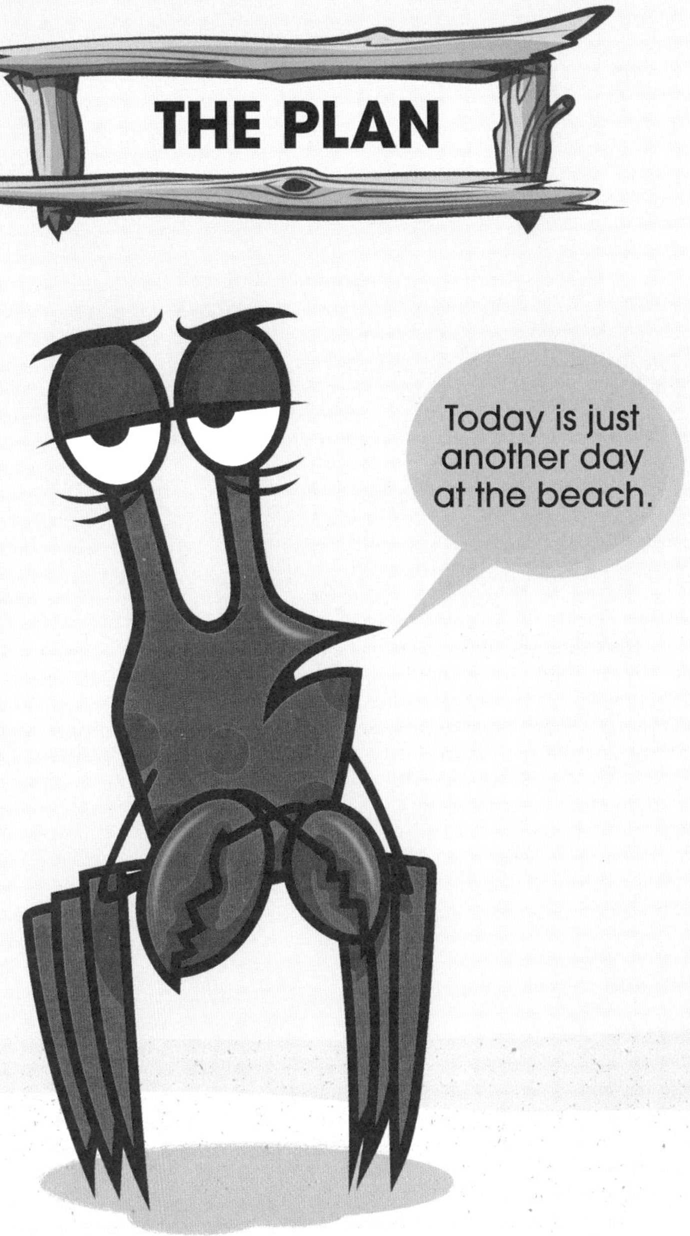
Today is just another day at the beach.

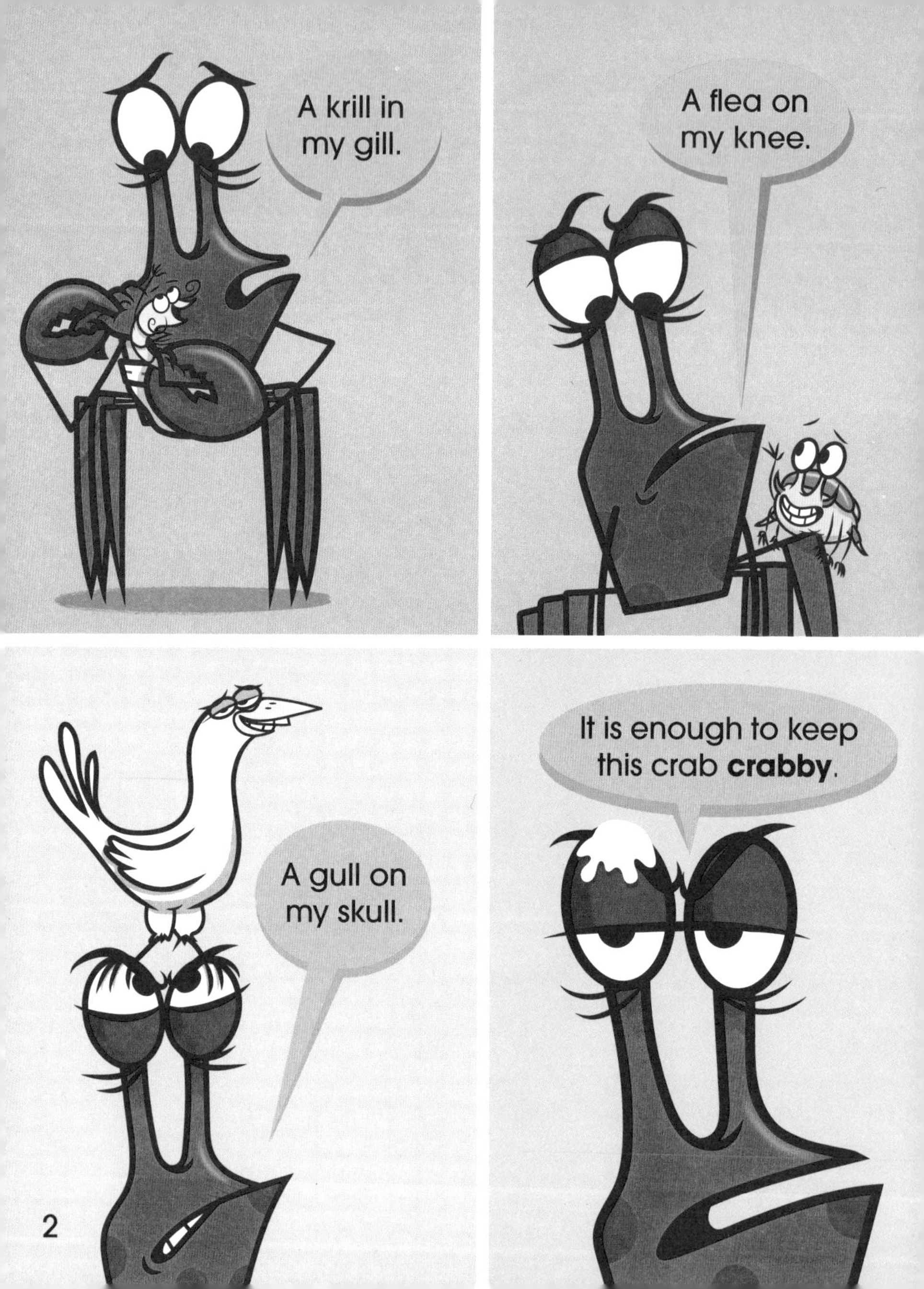
A krill in my gill.
A flea on my knee.
A gull on my skull.
It is enough to keep this crab **crabby**.

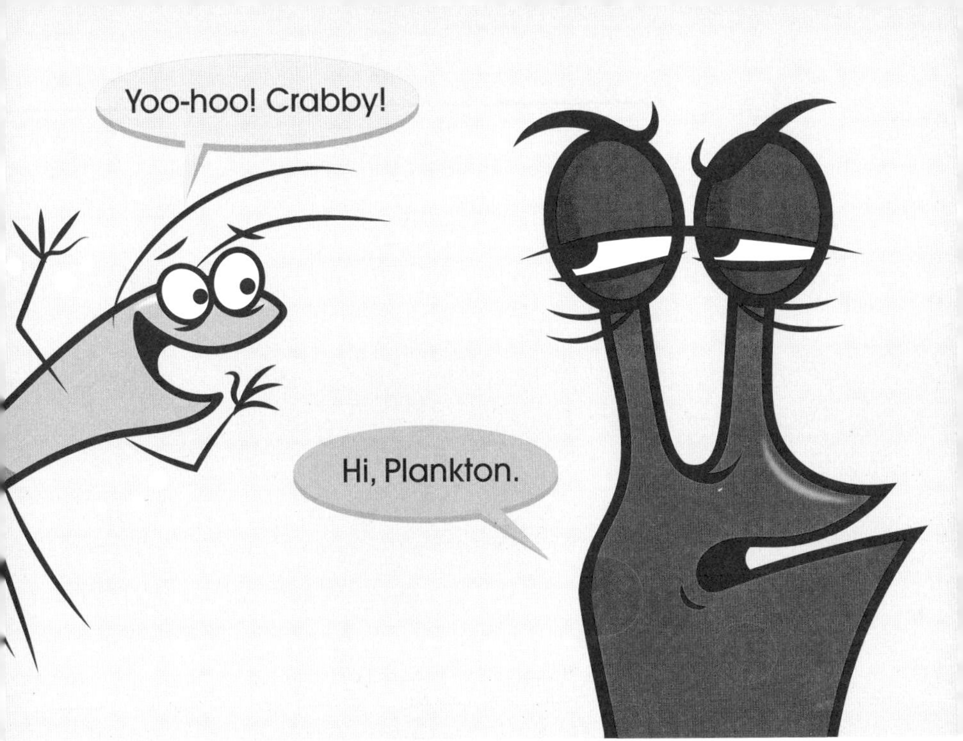
Yoo-hoo! Crabby!
Hi, Plankton.

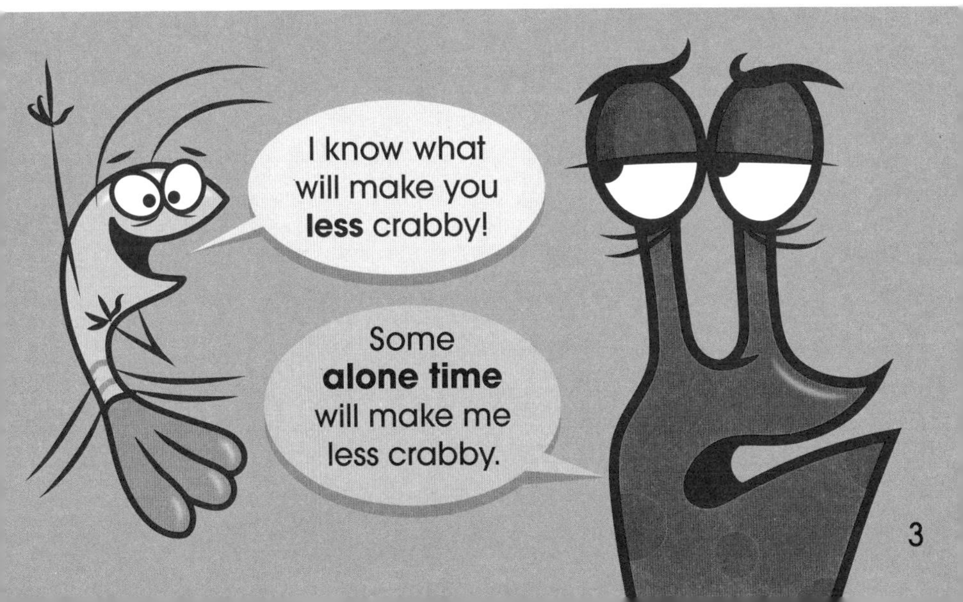
I know what will make you **less** crabby!
Some **alone time** will make me less crabby.

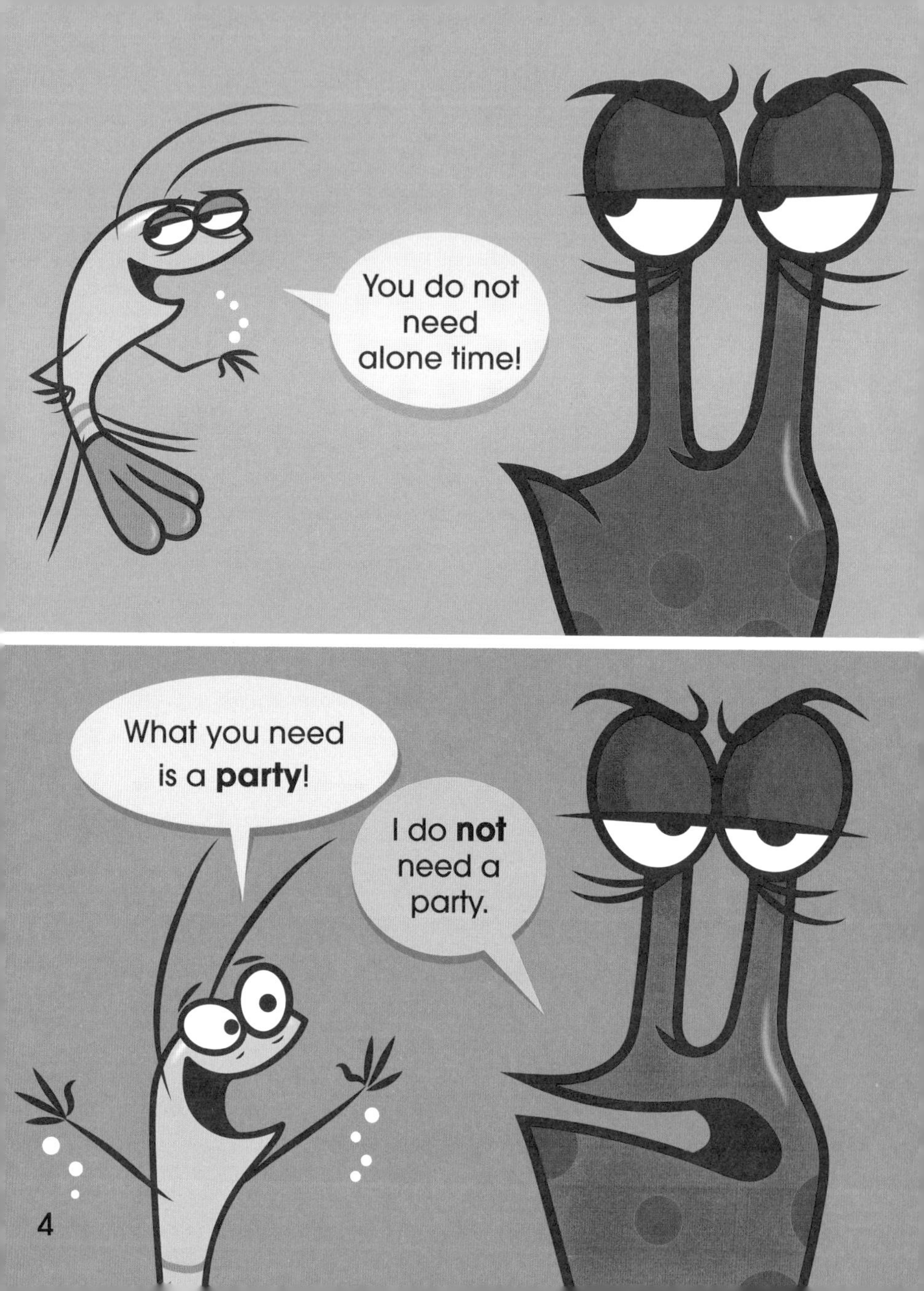
You do not need alone time!
What you need is a **party**!
I do **not** need a party.

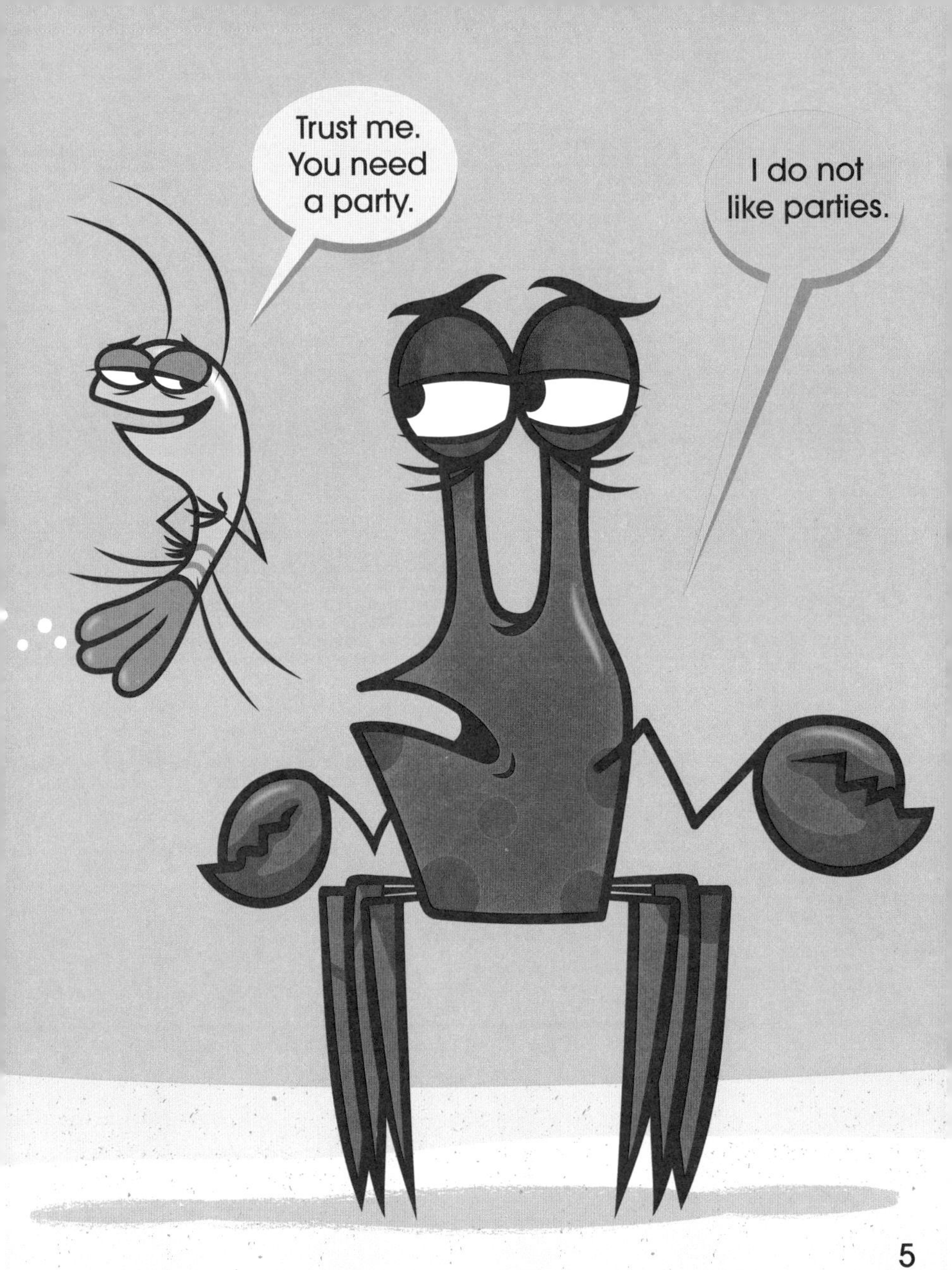
Trust me. You need a party.
I do not like parties.

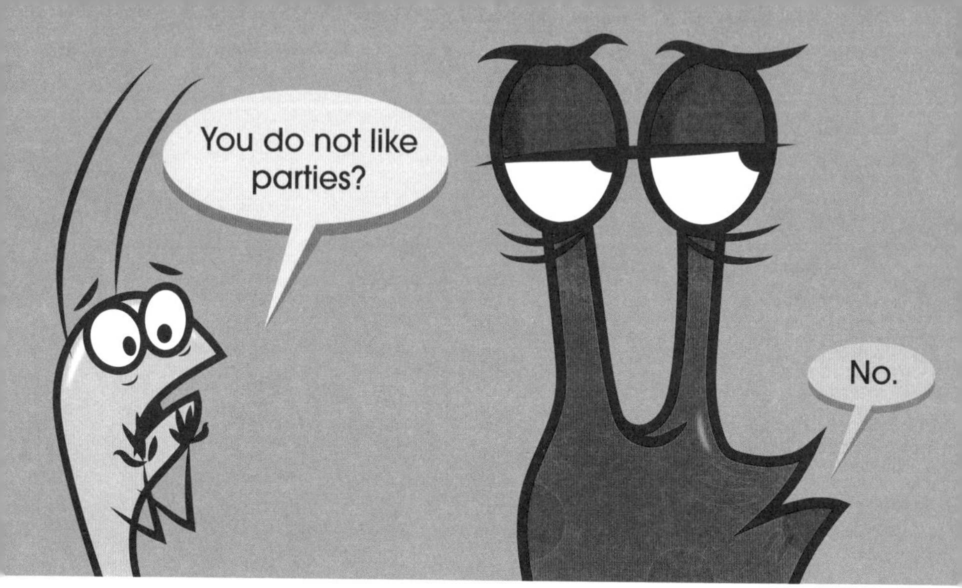
You do not like parties?
No.

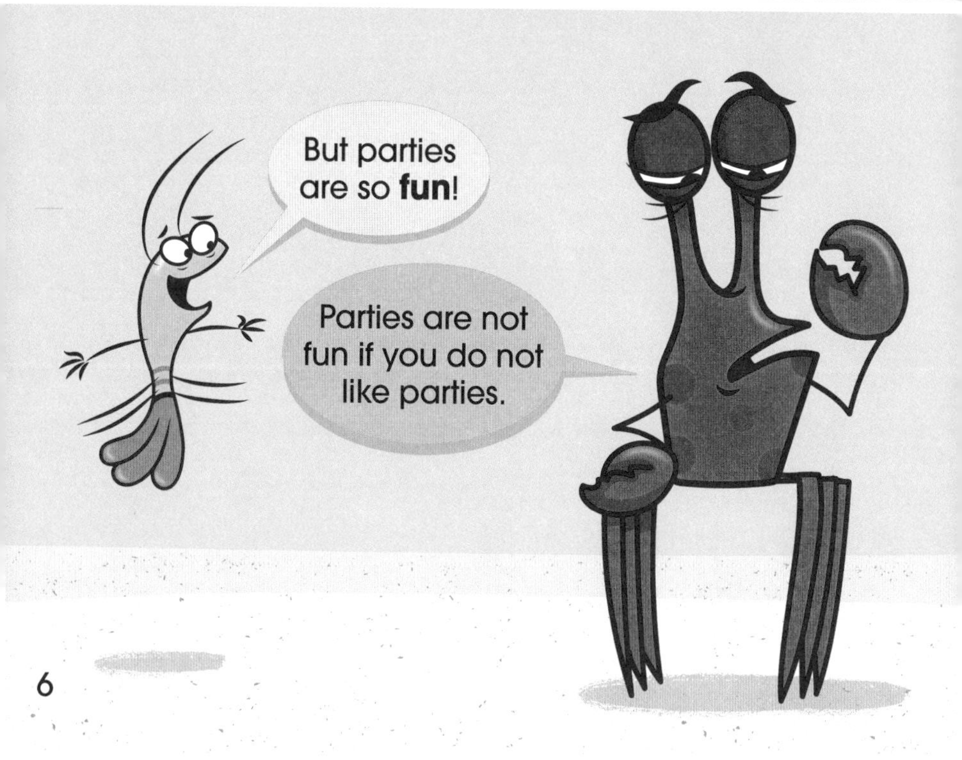
But parties are so **fun**!
Parties are not fun if you do not like parties.

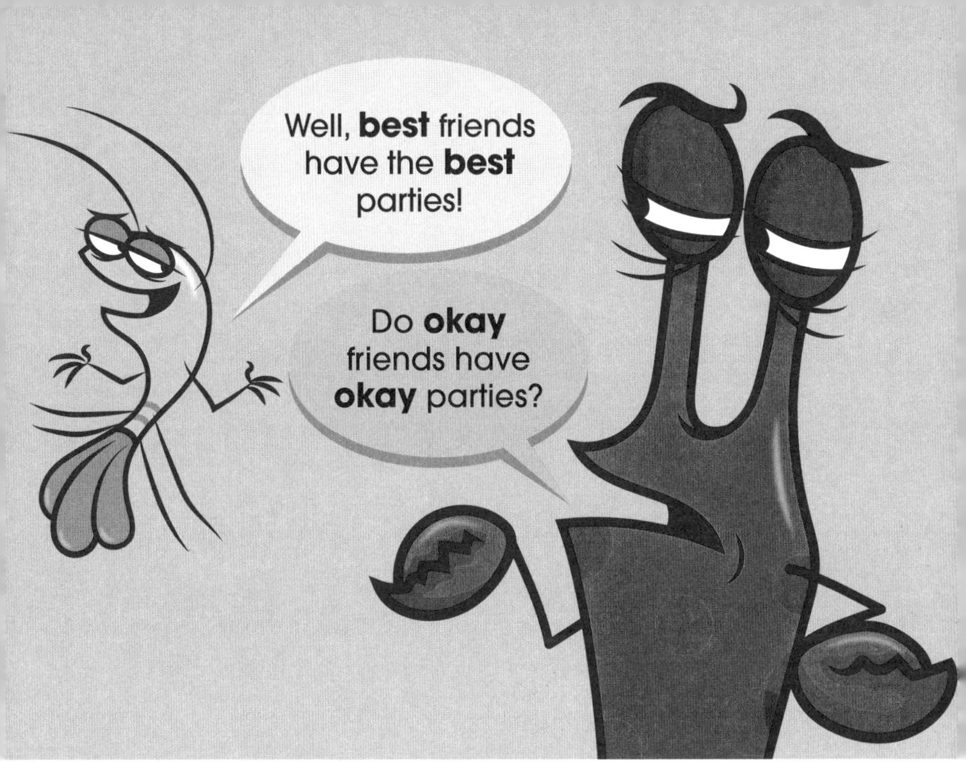
Well, best friends have the best parties!
Do okay friends have okay parties?

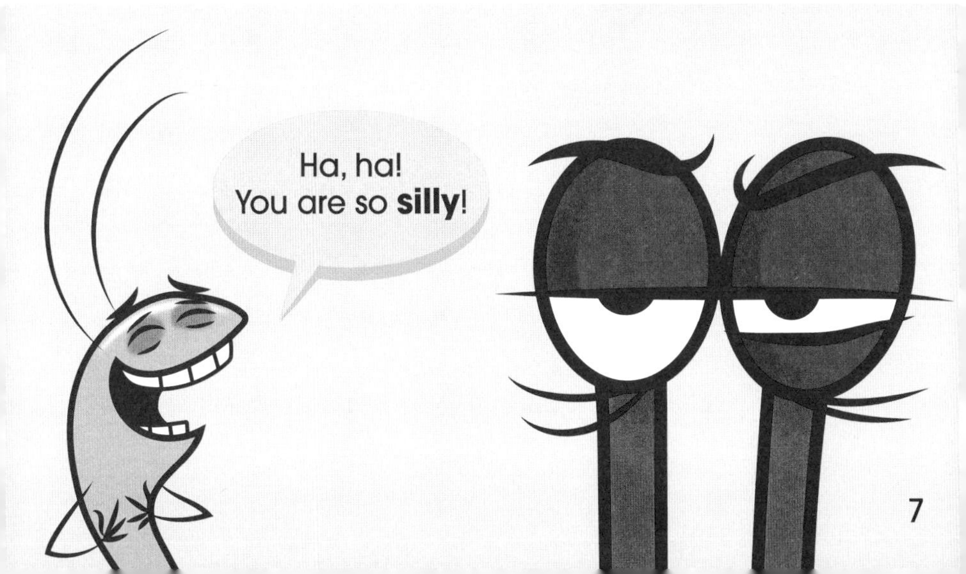
Ha, ha! You are so silly!

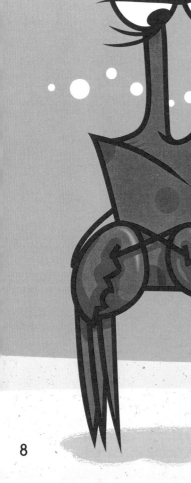

And what could be
more fun than a party
with my silly best friend?

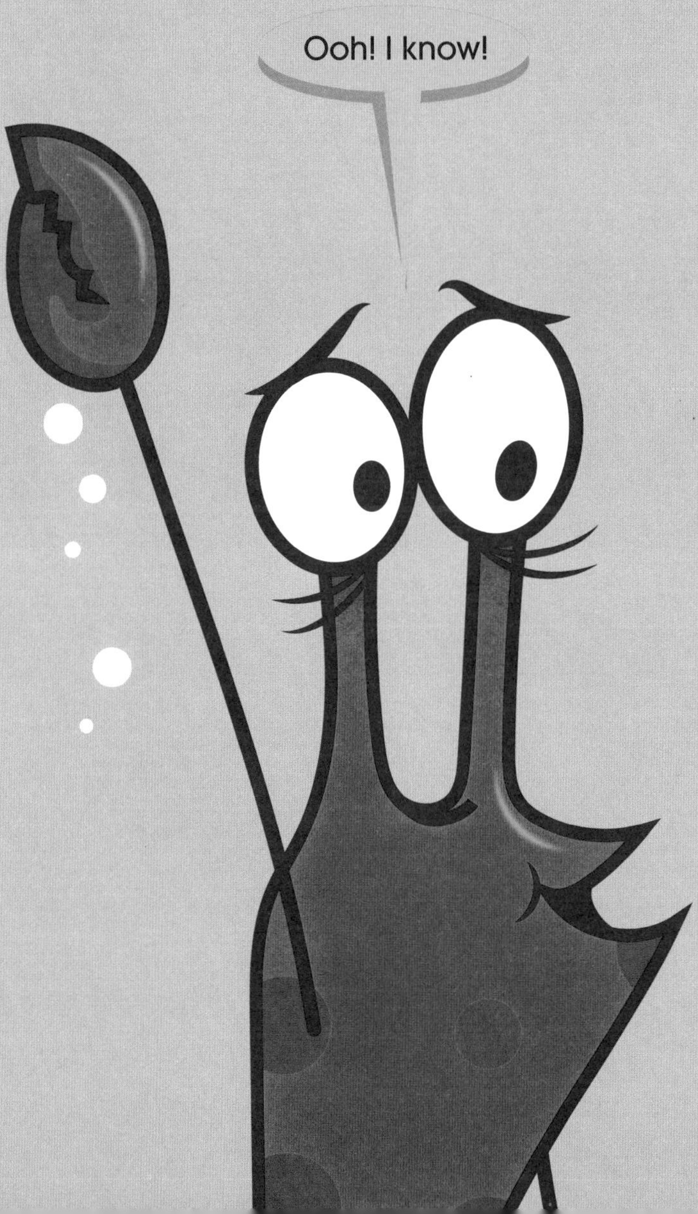
Ooh! I know!

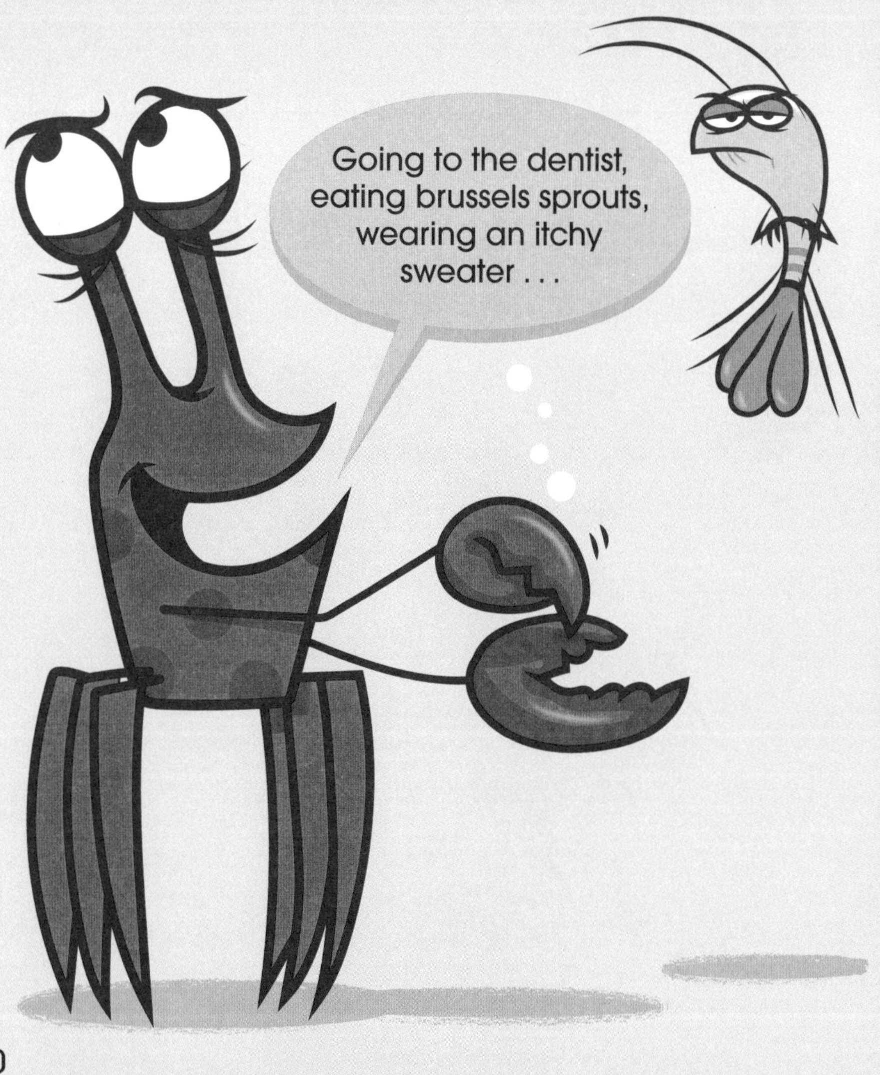
Going to the dentist, eating brussels sprouts, wearing an itchy sweater . . .

THE CARD

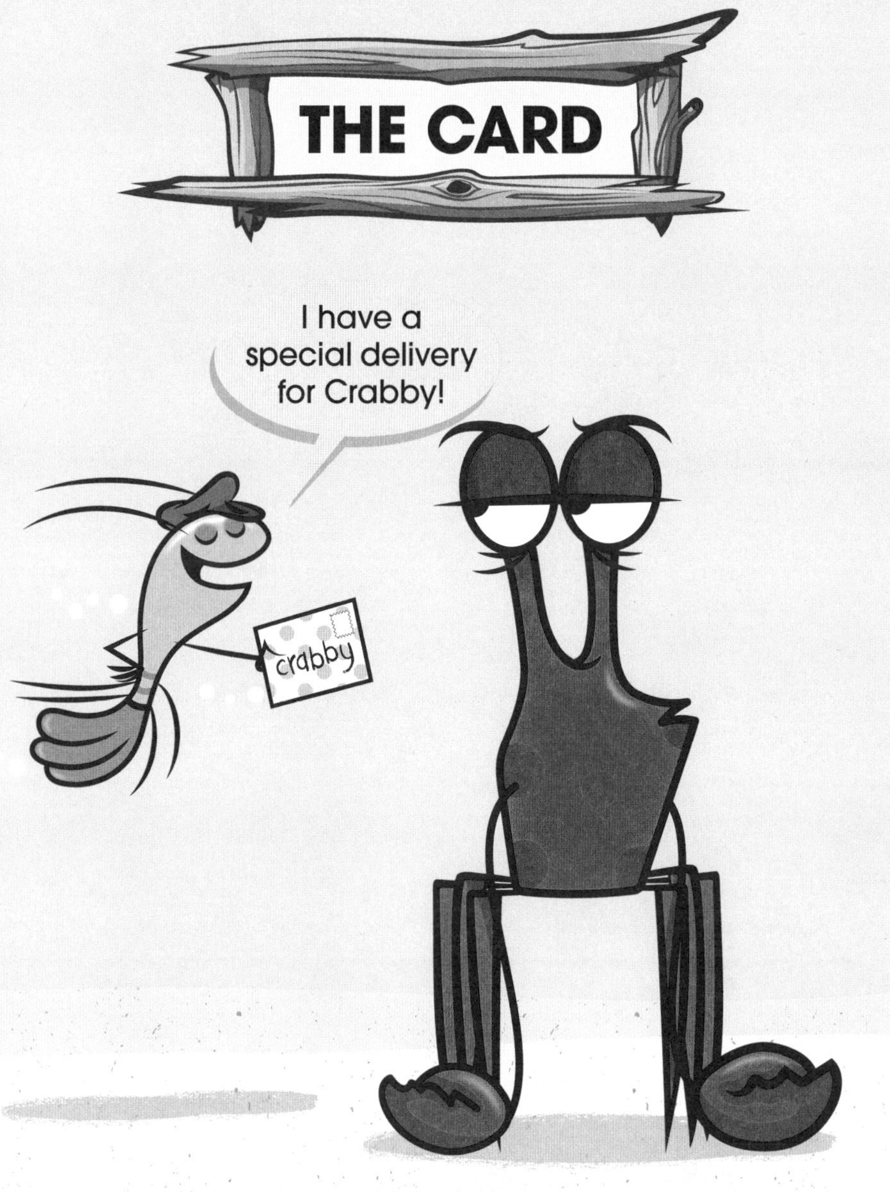
I have a special delivery for Crabby!
crabby

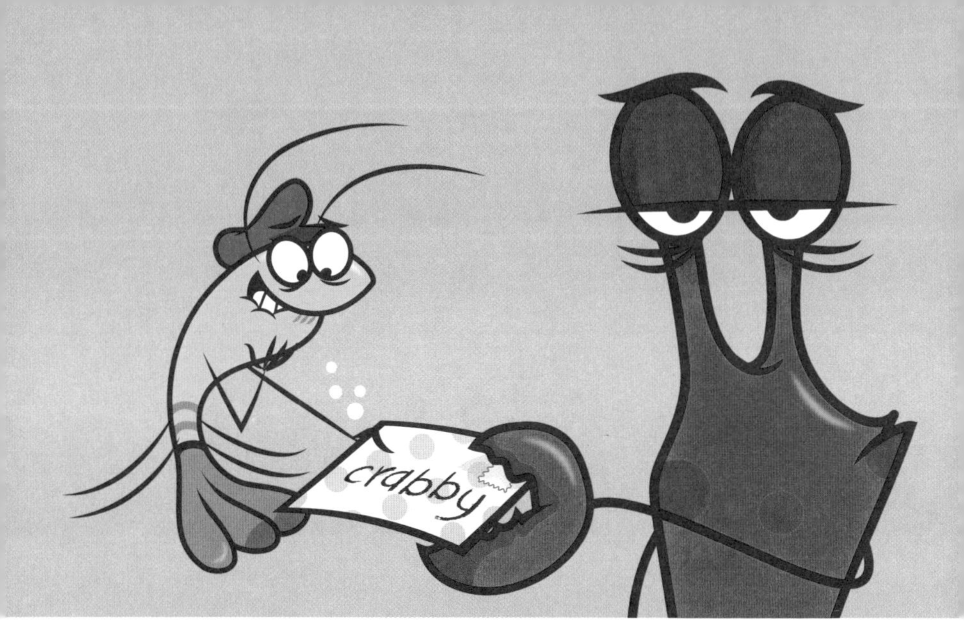
crabby

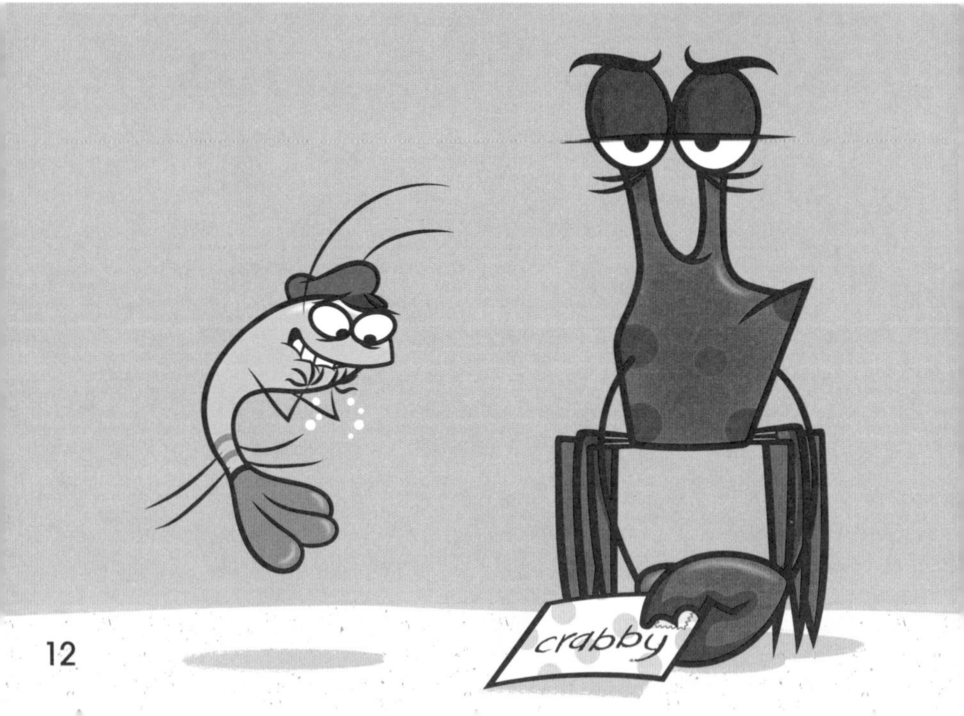
crabby

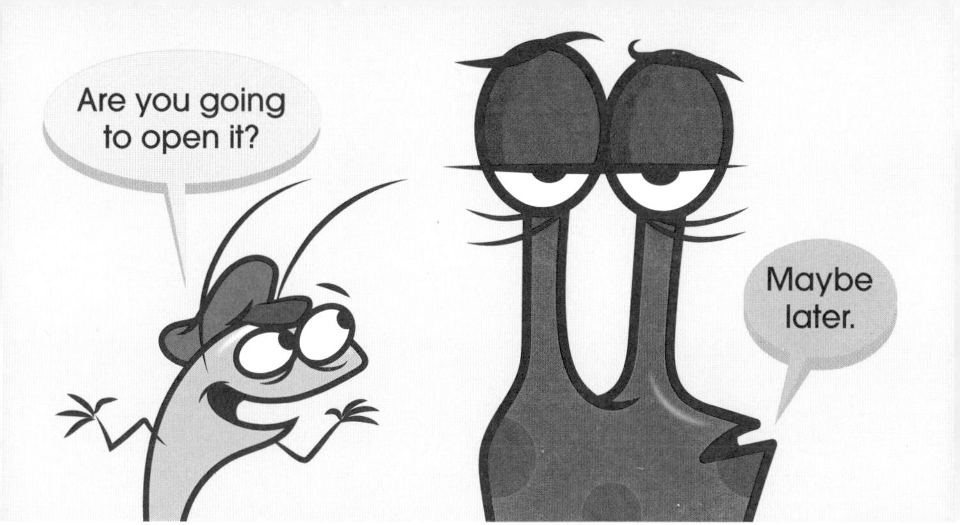
Are you going to open it?
Maybe later.

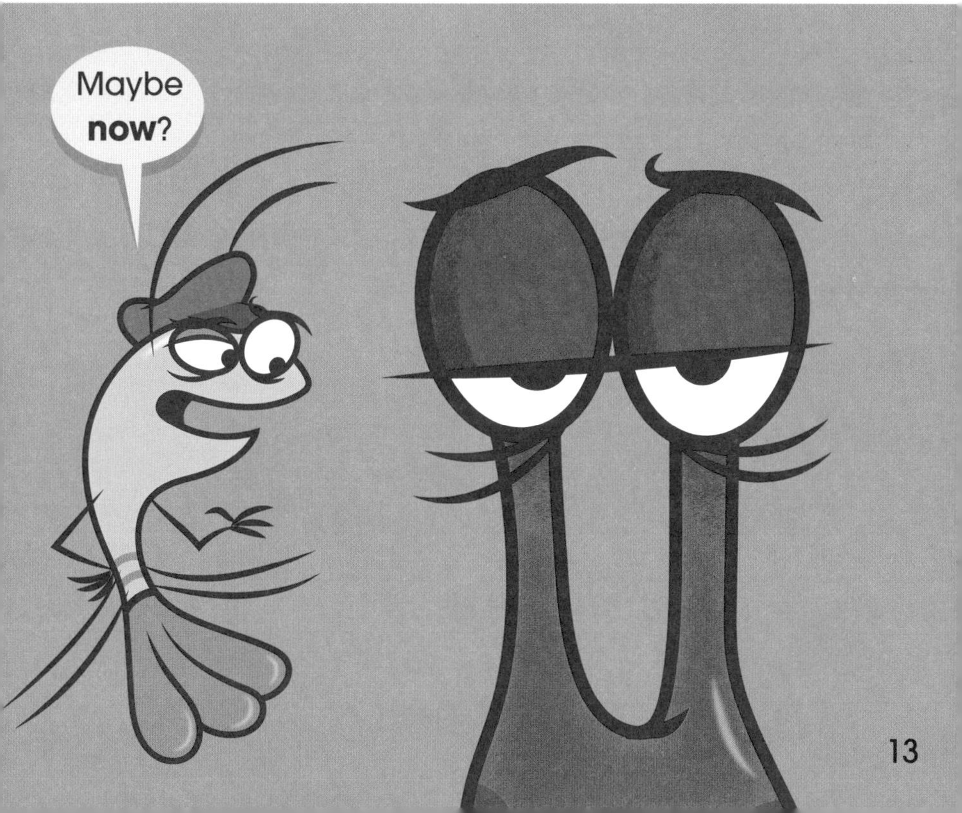
Maybe **now**?

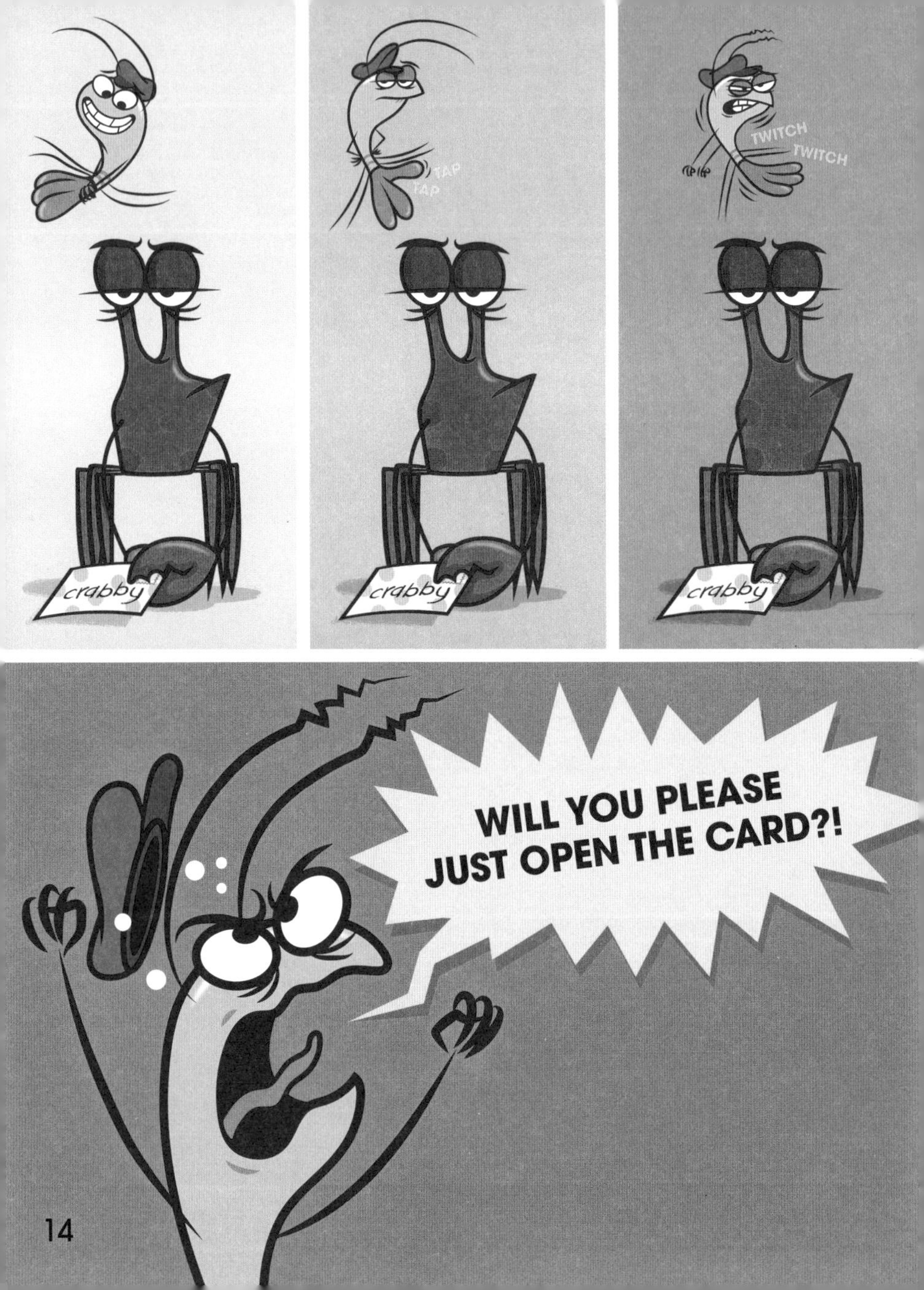
TAP
TAP
TWITCH
TWITCH
crabby
WILL YOU PLEASE JUST OPEN THE CARD?!

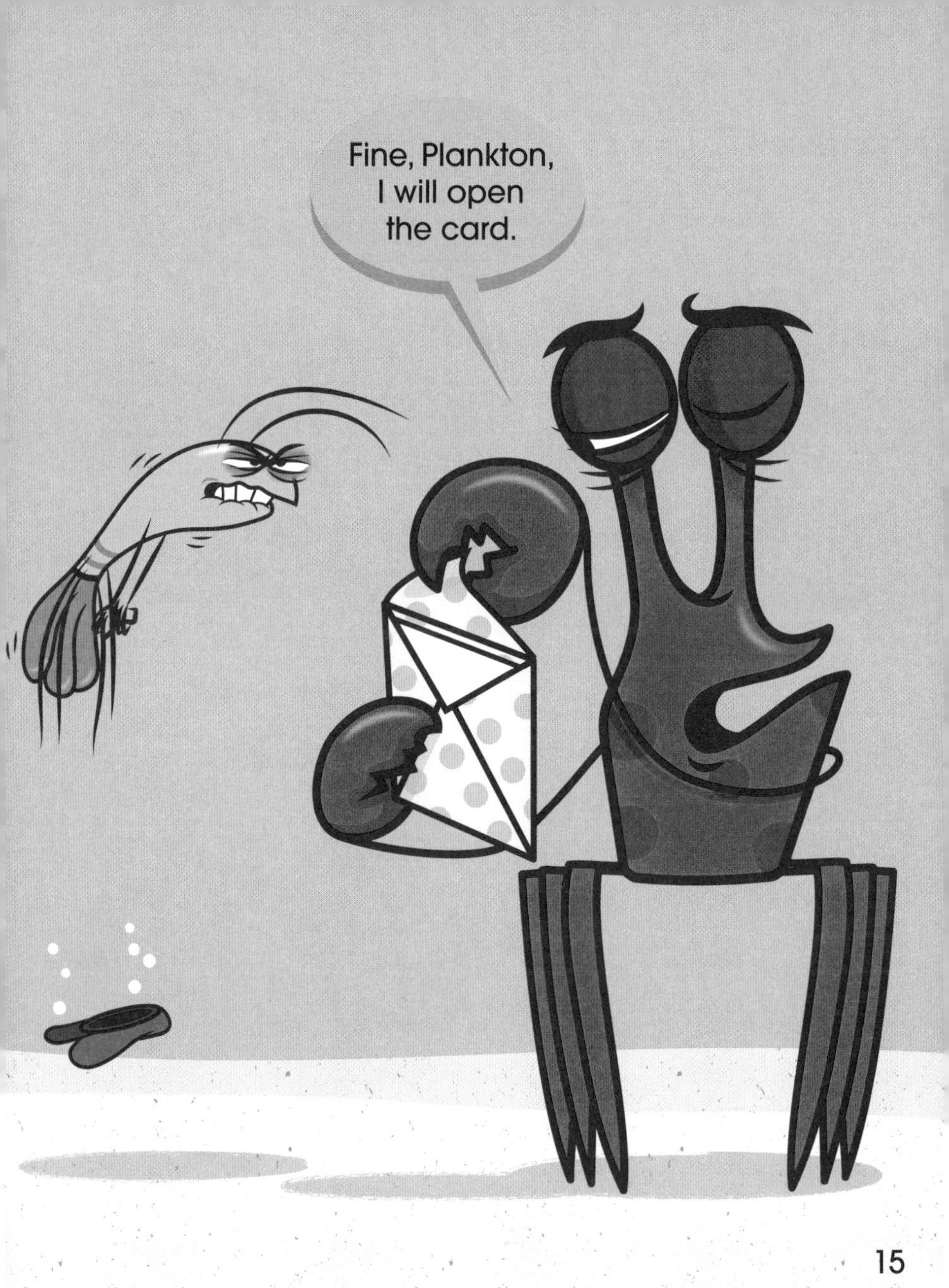
Fine, Plankton, I will open the card.

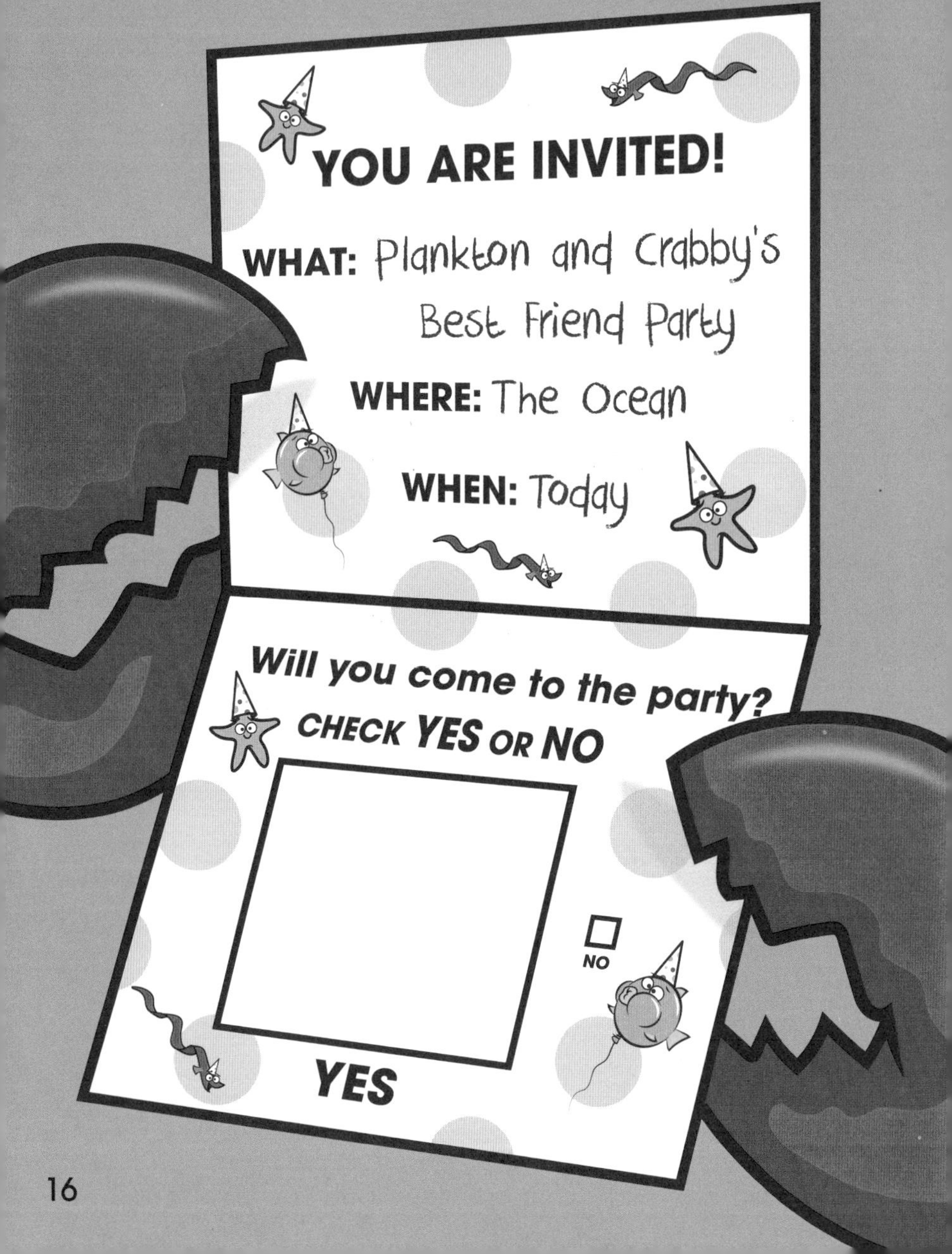
YOU ARE INVITED!
WHAT: Plankton and Crabby's Best Friend Party
WHERE: The Ocean
WHEN: Today
Will you come to the party?
CHECK YES OR NO
NO
YES

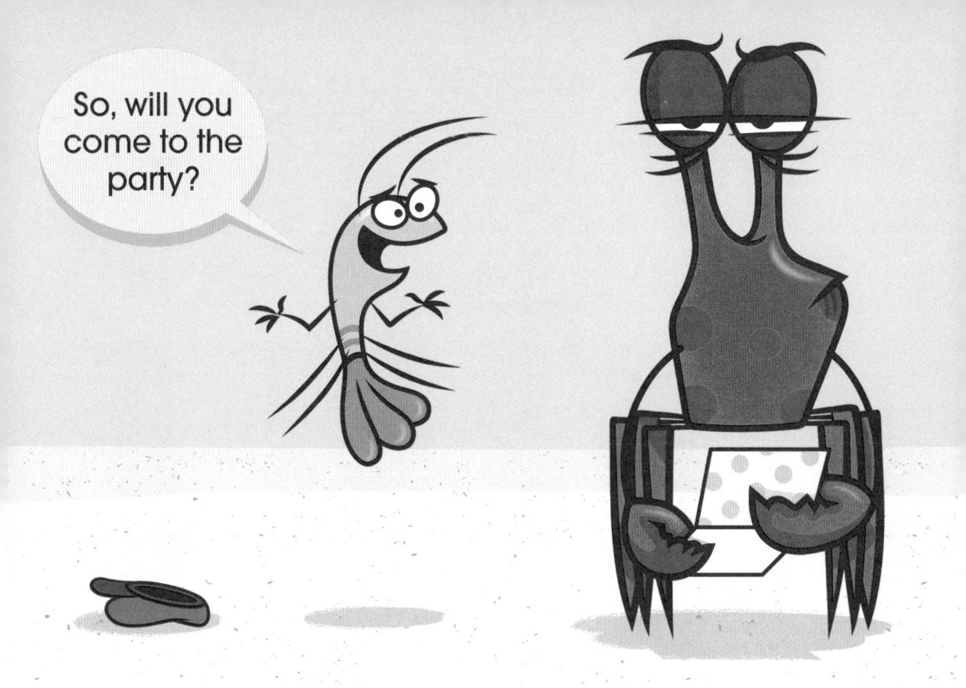
So, will you come to the party?

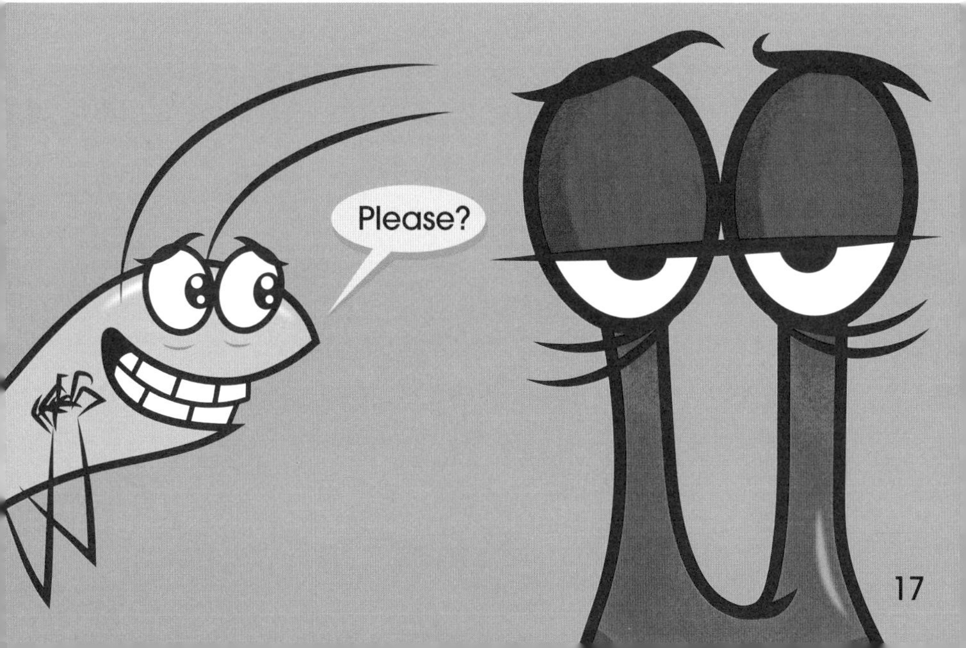
Please?

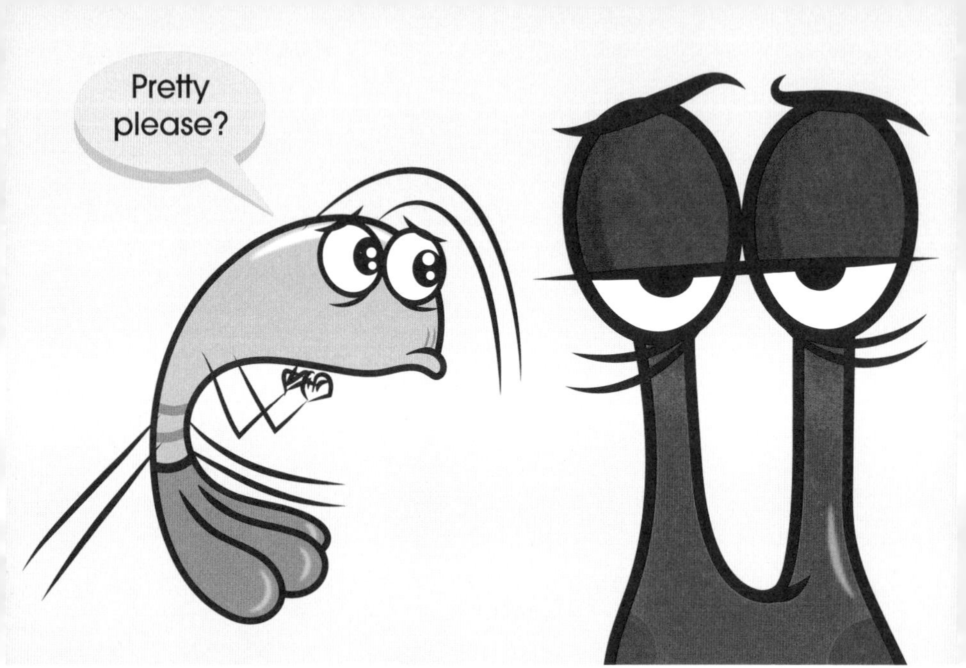
Pretty please?

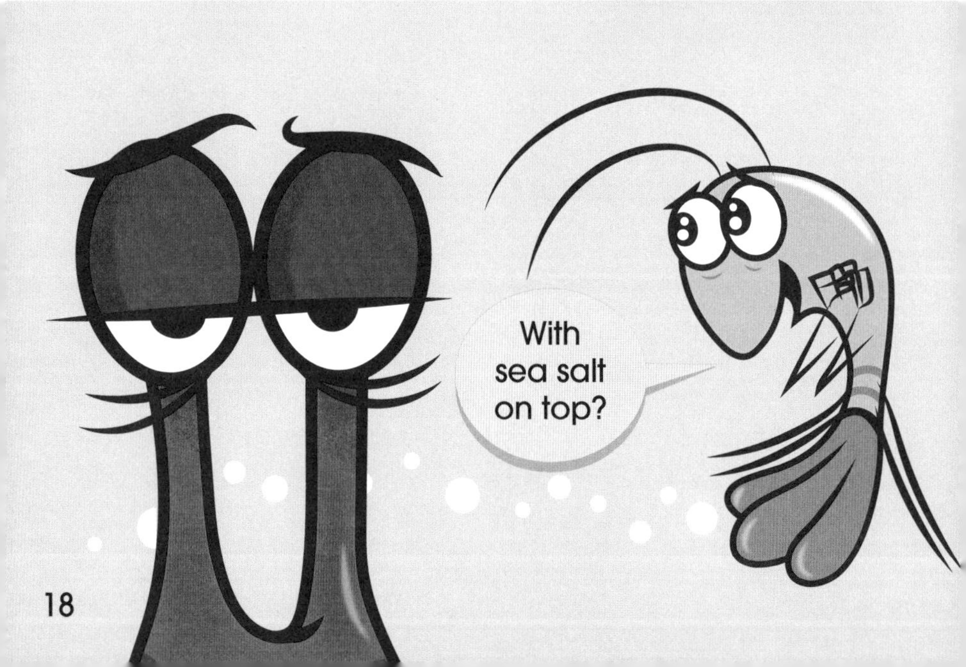
With sea salt on top?

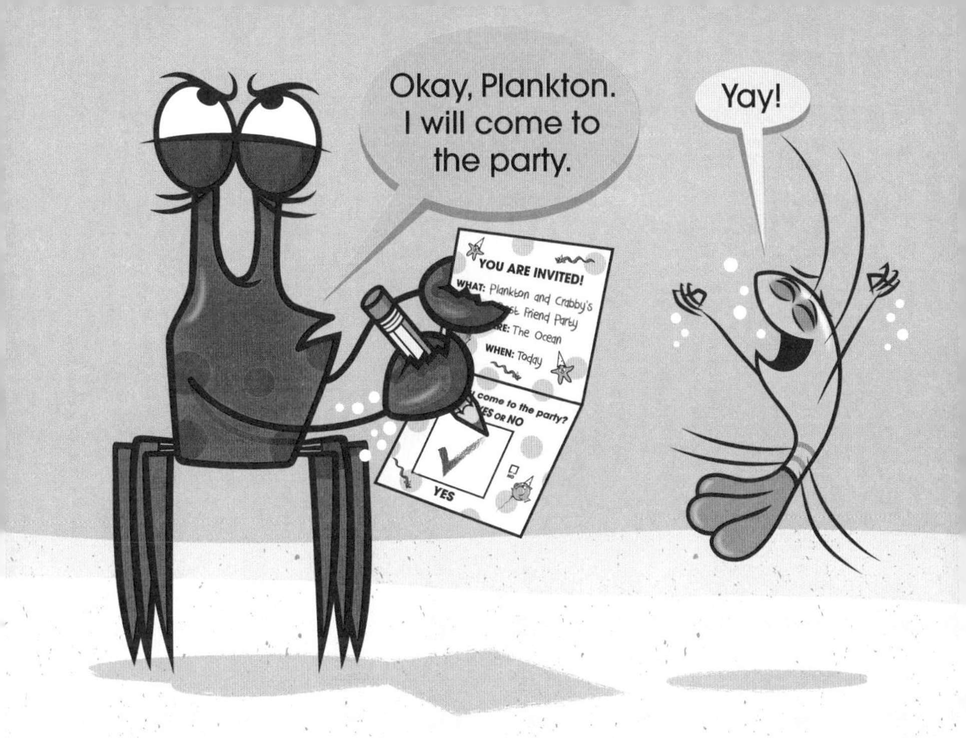
Okay, Plankton. I will come to the party.
Yay!
YOU ARE INVITED!
WHEN: Today
YES

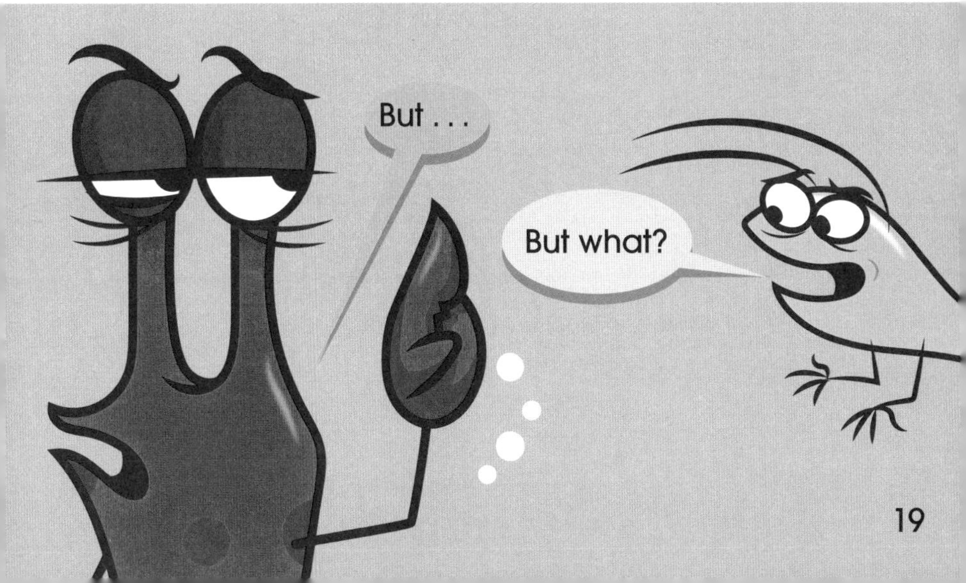
But . . .
But what?

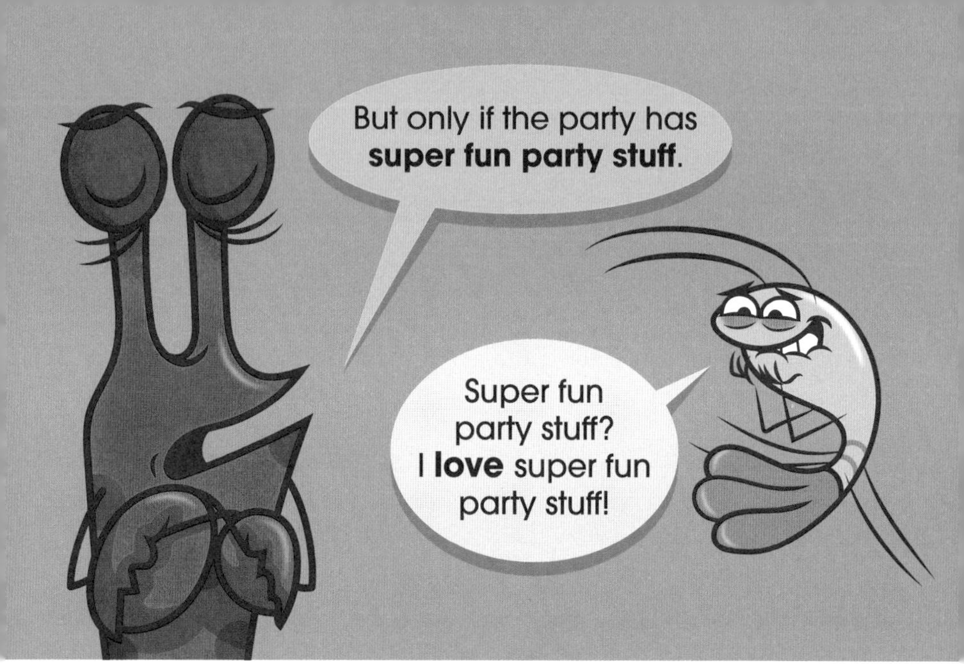
But only if the party has **super fun party stuff**.
Super fun party stuff? I **love** super fun party stuff!

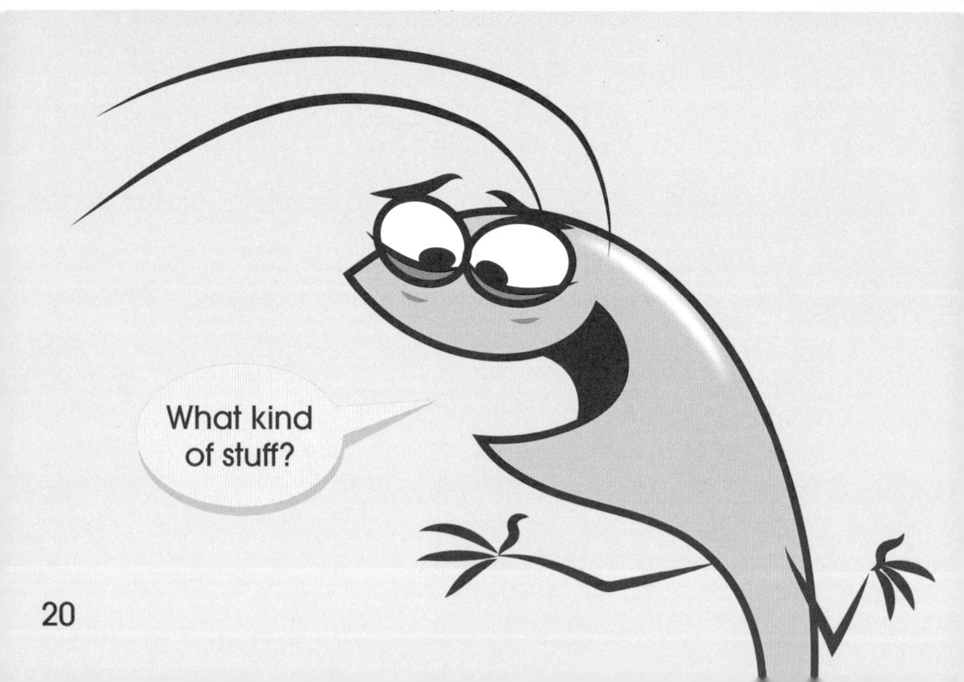
What kind of stuff?

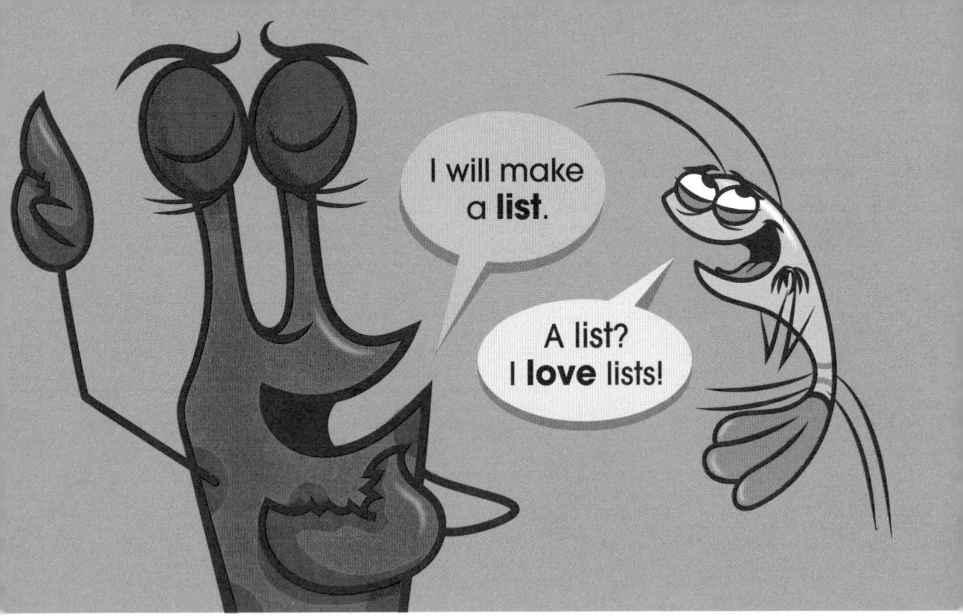
I will make a **list**.
A list? I **love** lists!

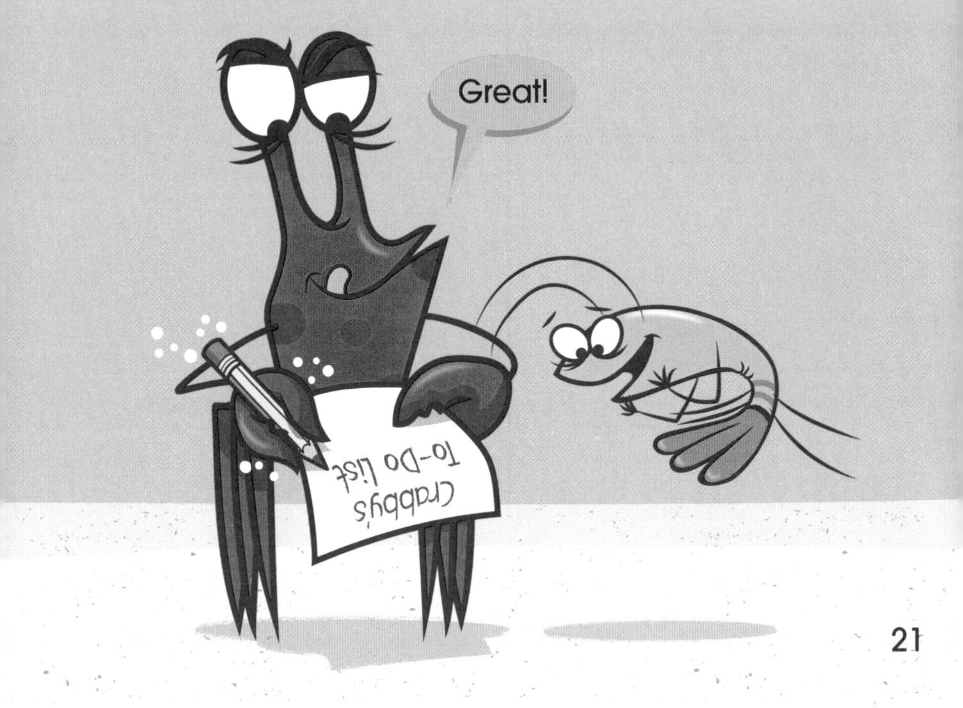
Great!
Crabby's To-Do List

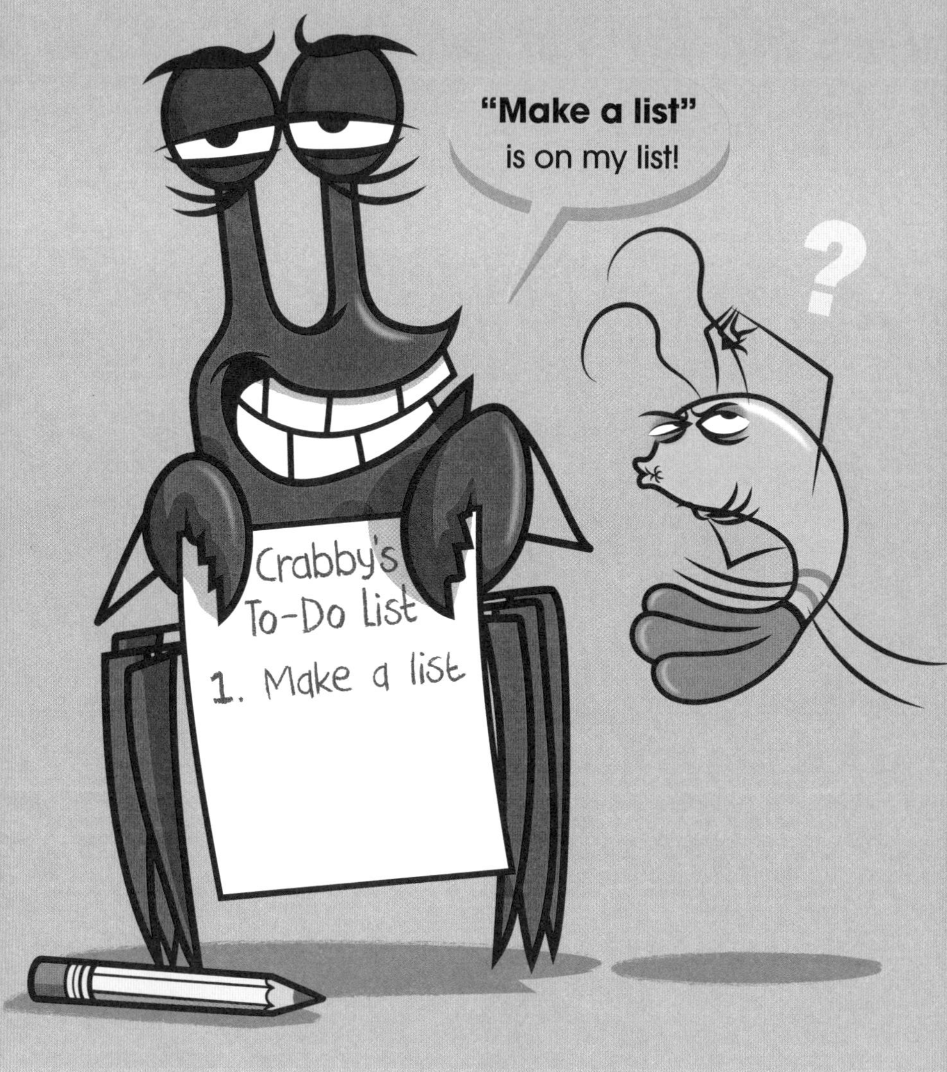
"Make a list"
is on my list!
?
Crabby's
To-Do List
1. Make a list

THE LIST

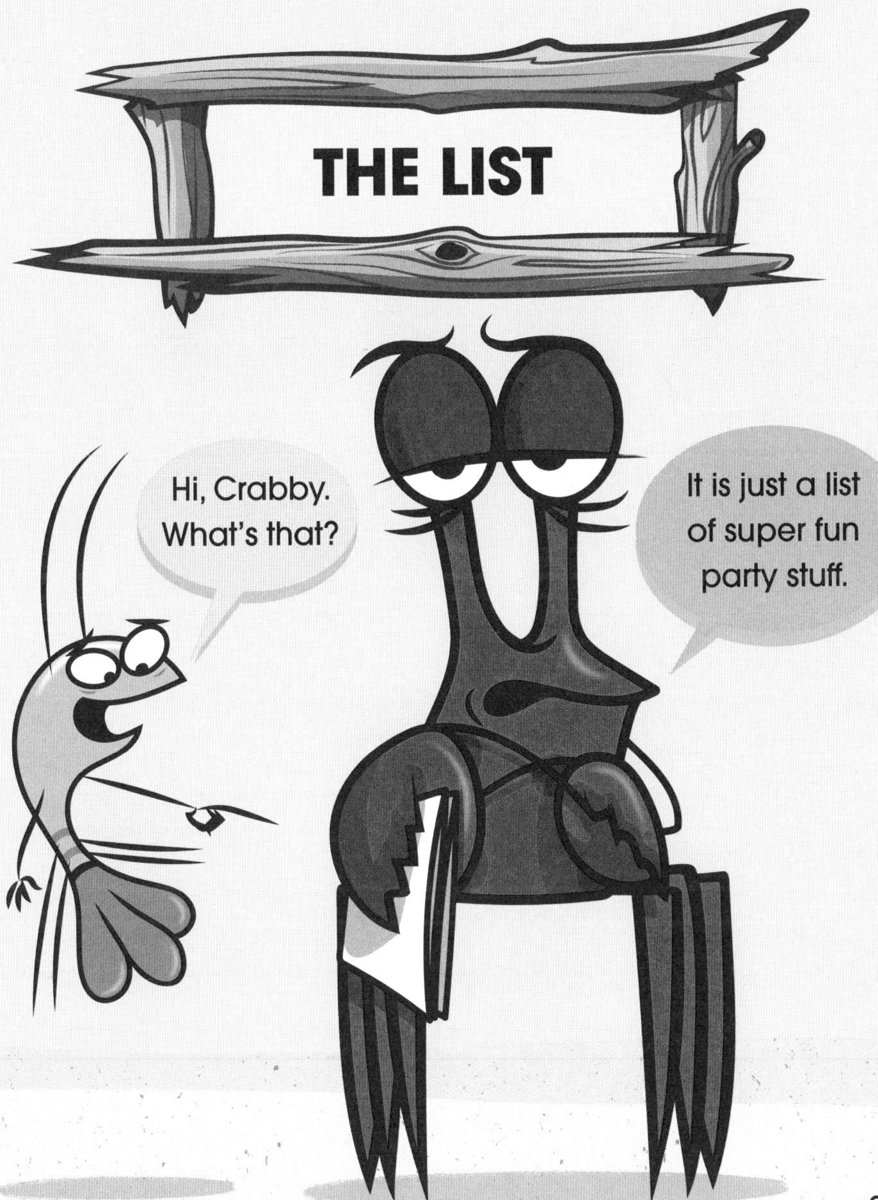
Hi, Crabby. What's that?
It is just a list of super fun party stuff.

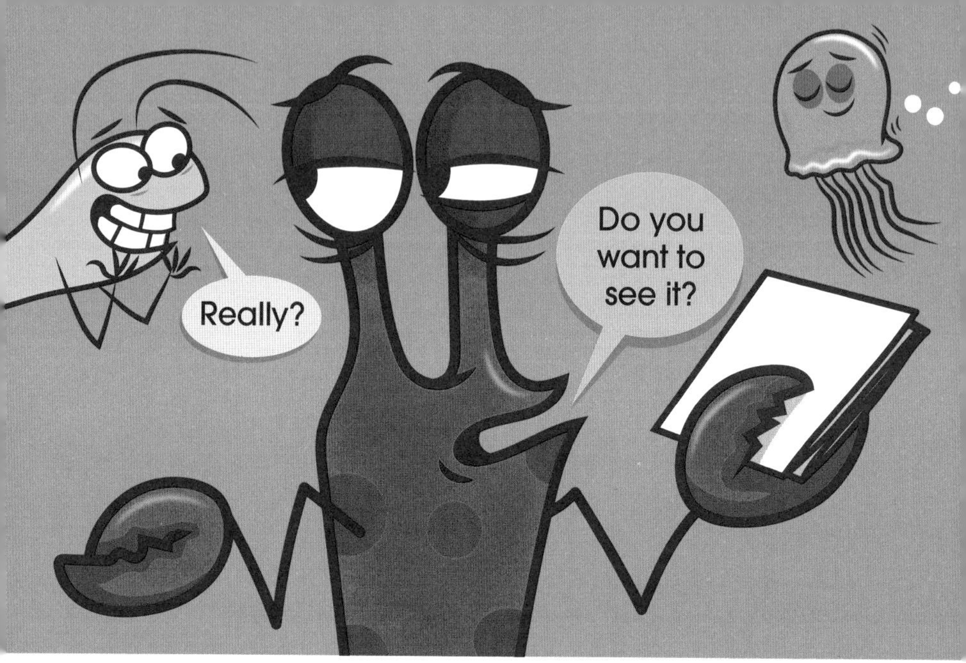
Really?
Do you want to see it?

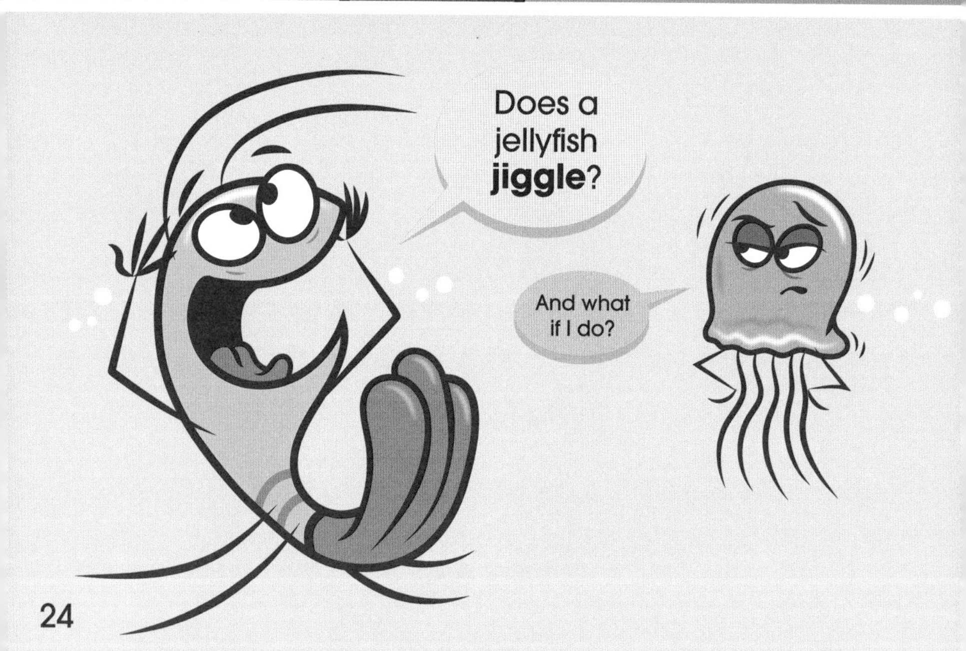
Does a jellyfish **jiggle**?
And what if I do?

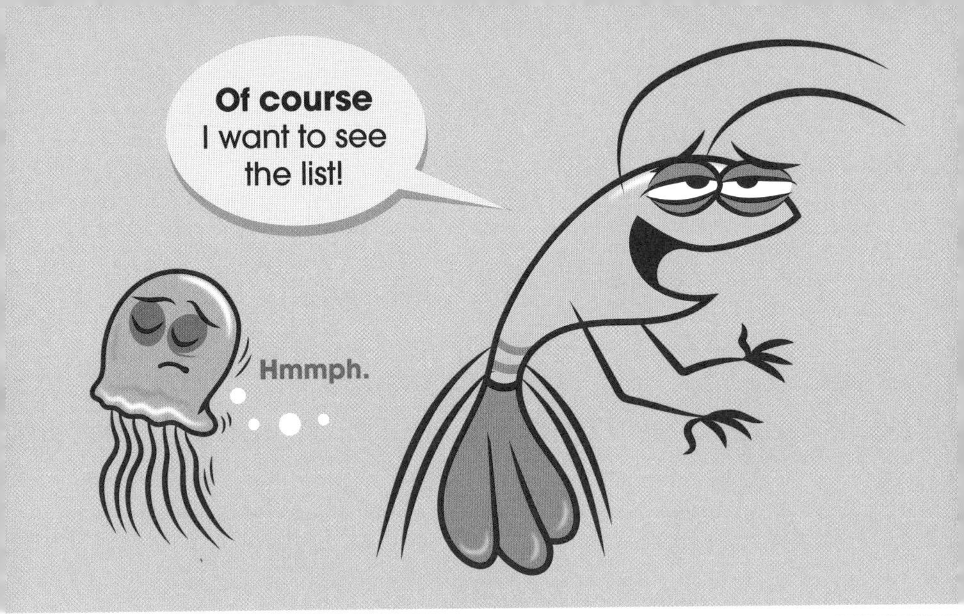
Of course
I want to see
the list!
Hmmph.

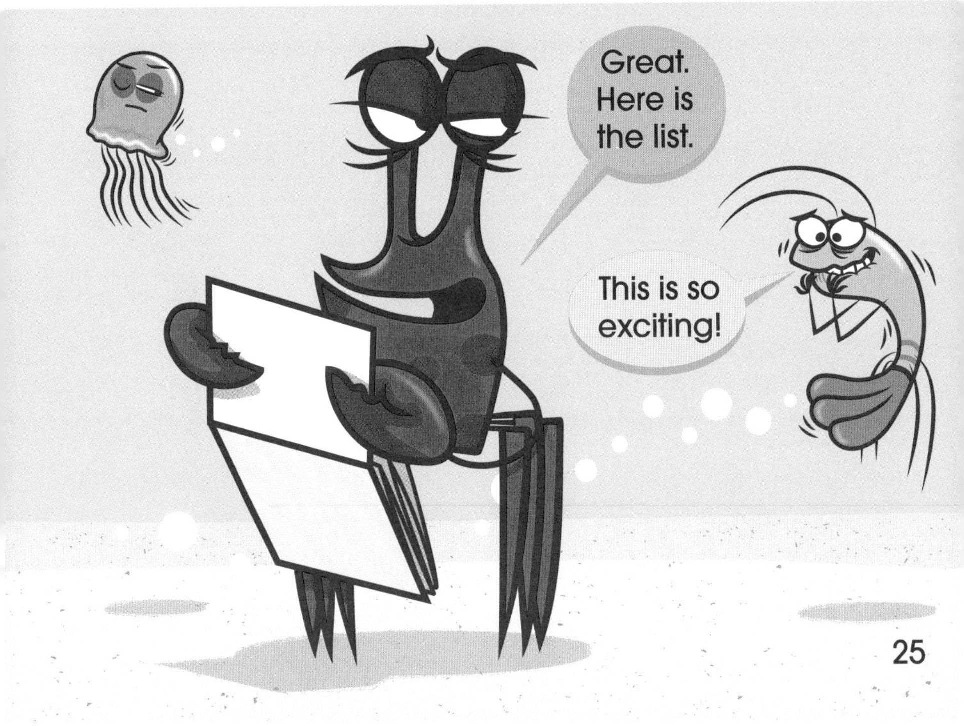
Great.
Here is
the list.
This is so
exciting!

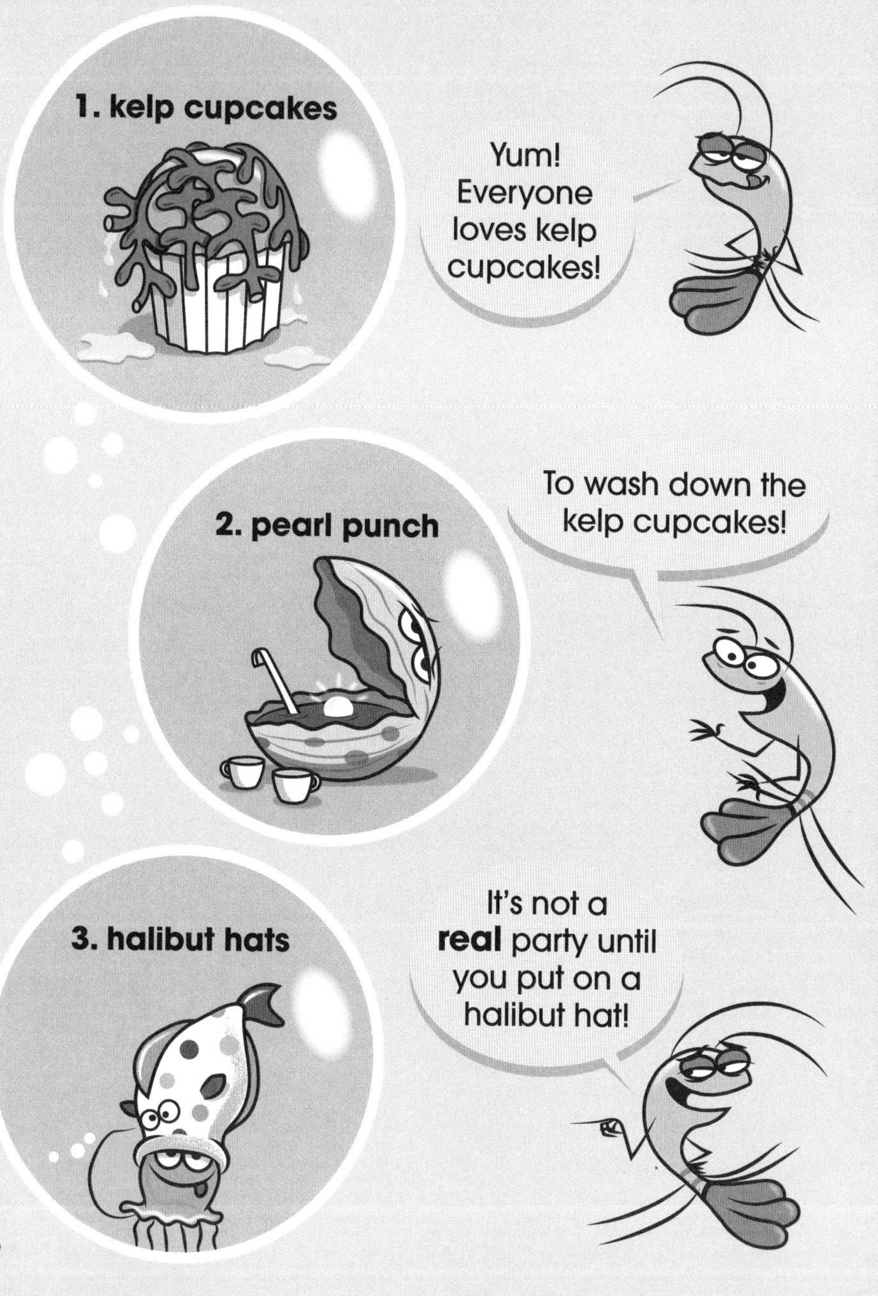
1. kelp cupcakes
Yum! Everyone loves kelp cupcakes!
2. pearl punch
To wash down the kelp cupcakes!
3. halibut hats
It's not a **real** party until you put on a halibut hat!

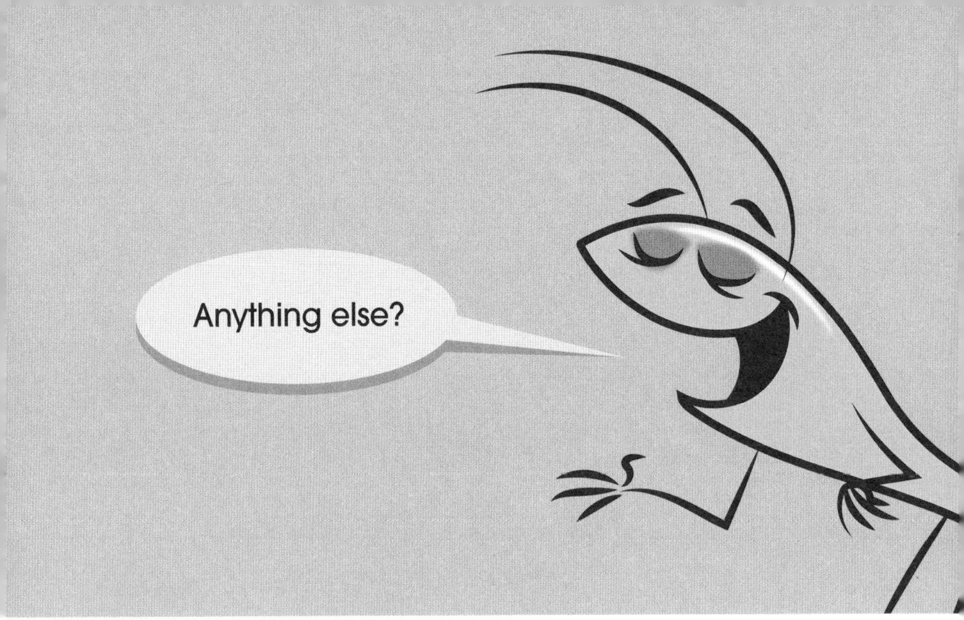
Anything else?

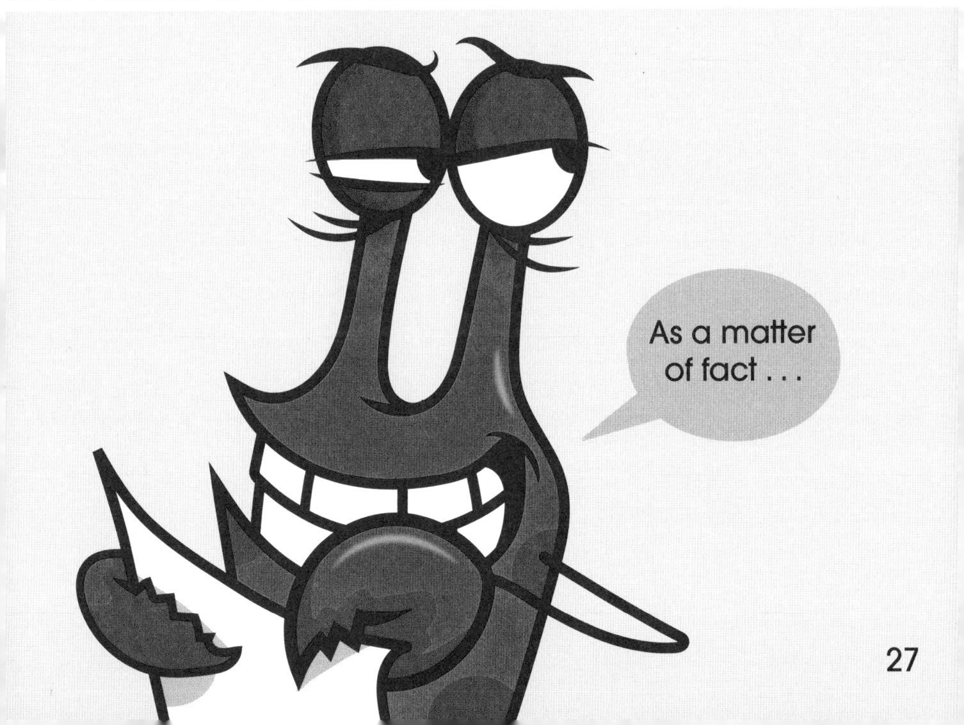
As a matter
of fact . . .

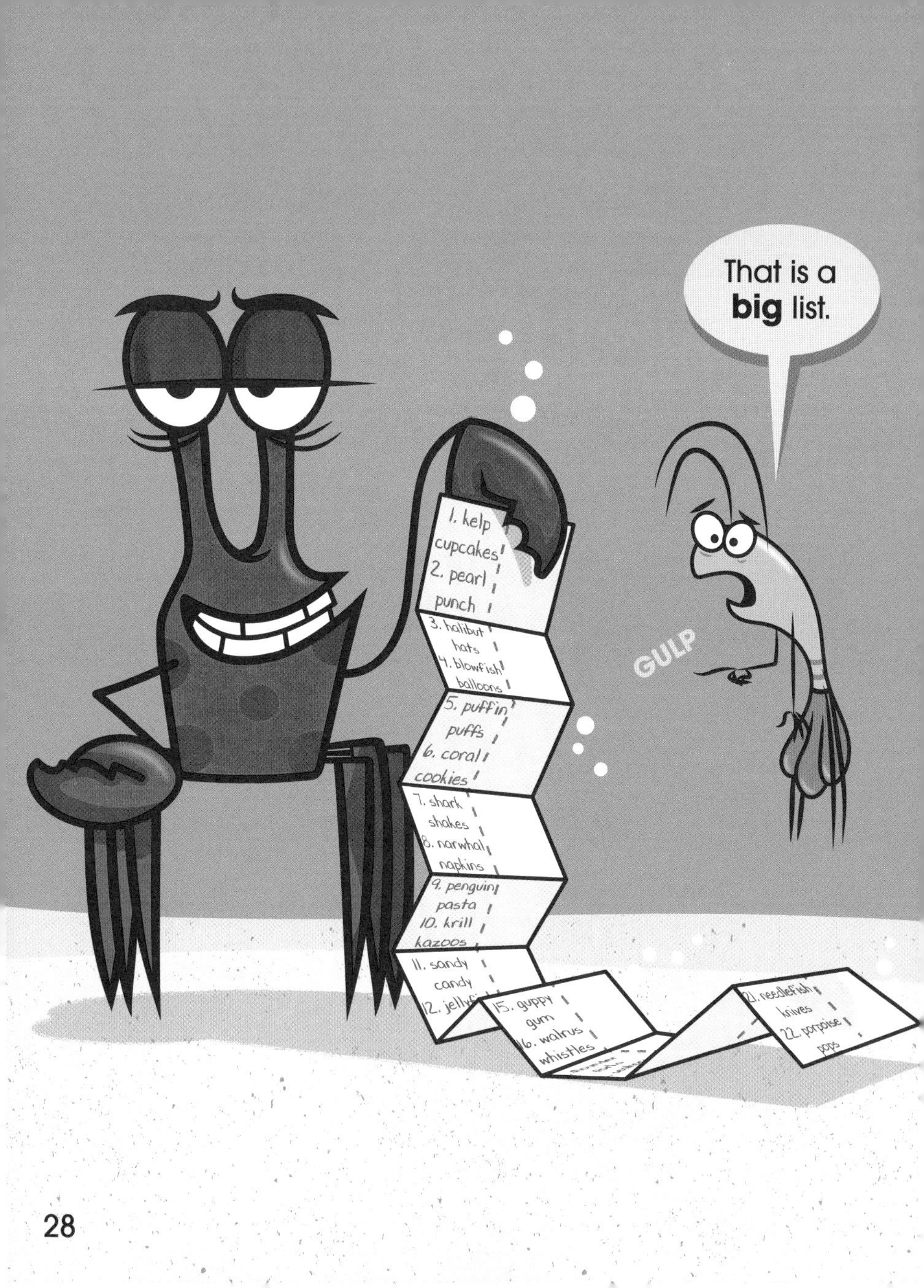
That is a **big** list.
GULP
1. kelp cupcakes
2. pearl punch
3. halibut hats
4. blowfish balloons
5. puffin puffs
6. coral cookies
7. shark shakes
8. narwhal napkins
9. penguin pasta
10. krill kazoos
11. sandy candy
15. guppy gum
16. walrus whistles
21. needlefish knives
22. porpoise pops

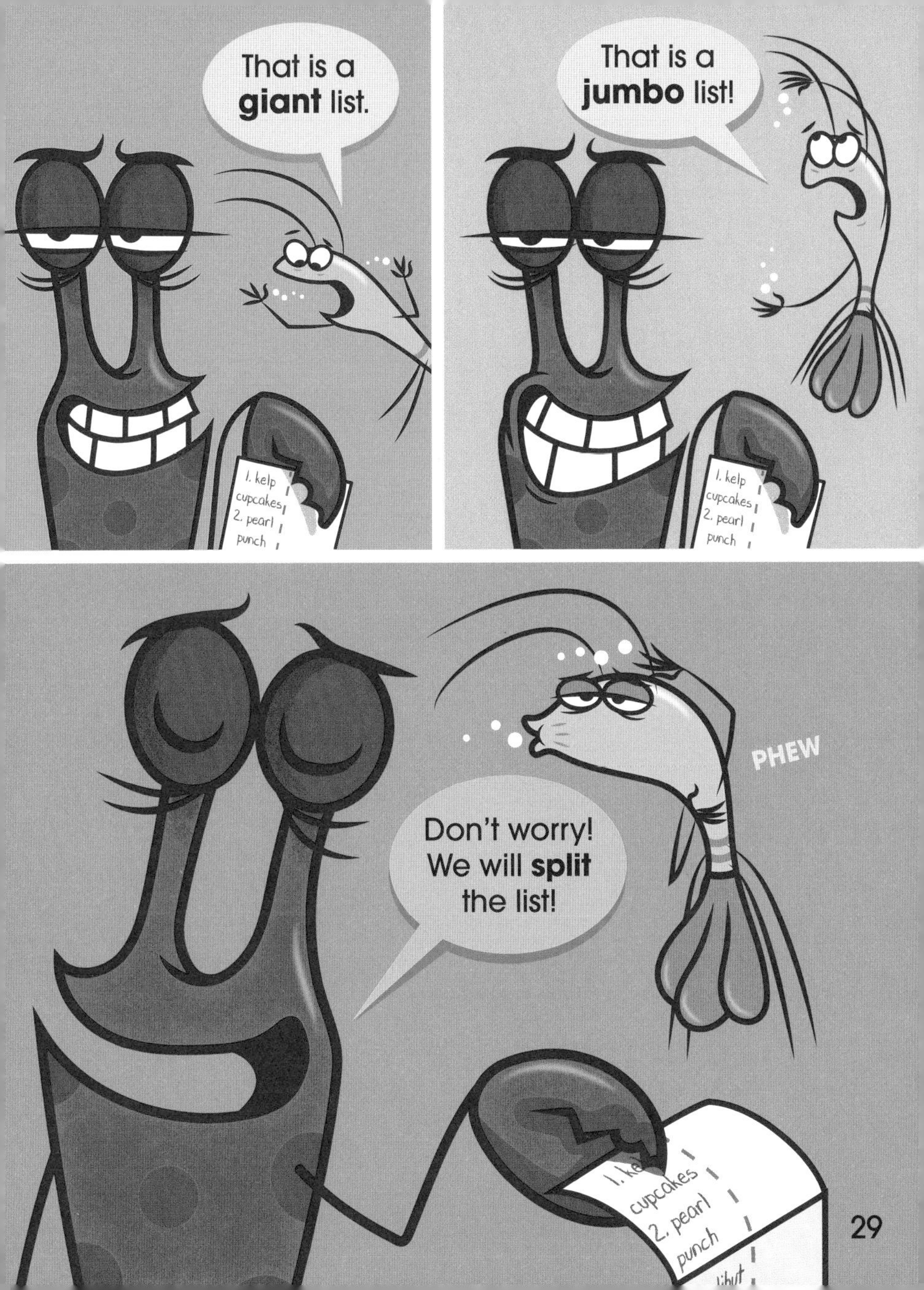
That is a **giant** list.
1. kelp cupcakes 2. pearl punch
That is a **jumbo** list!
1. kelp cupcakes 2. pearl punch
PHEW
Don't worry! We will **split** the list!
cupcakes 2. pearl punch

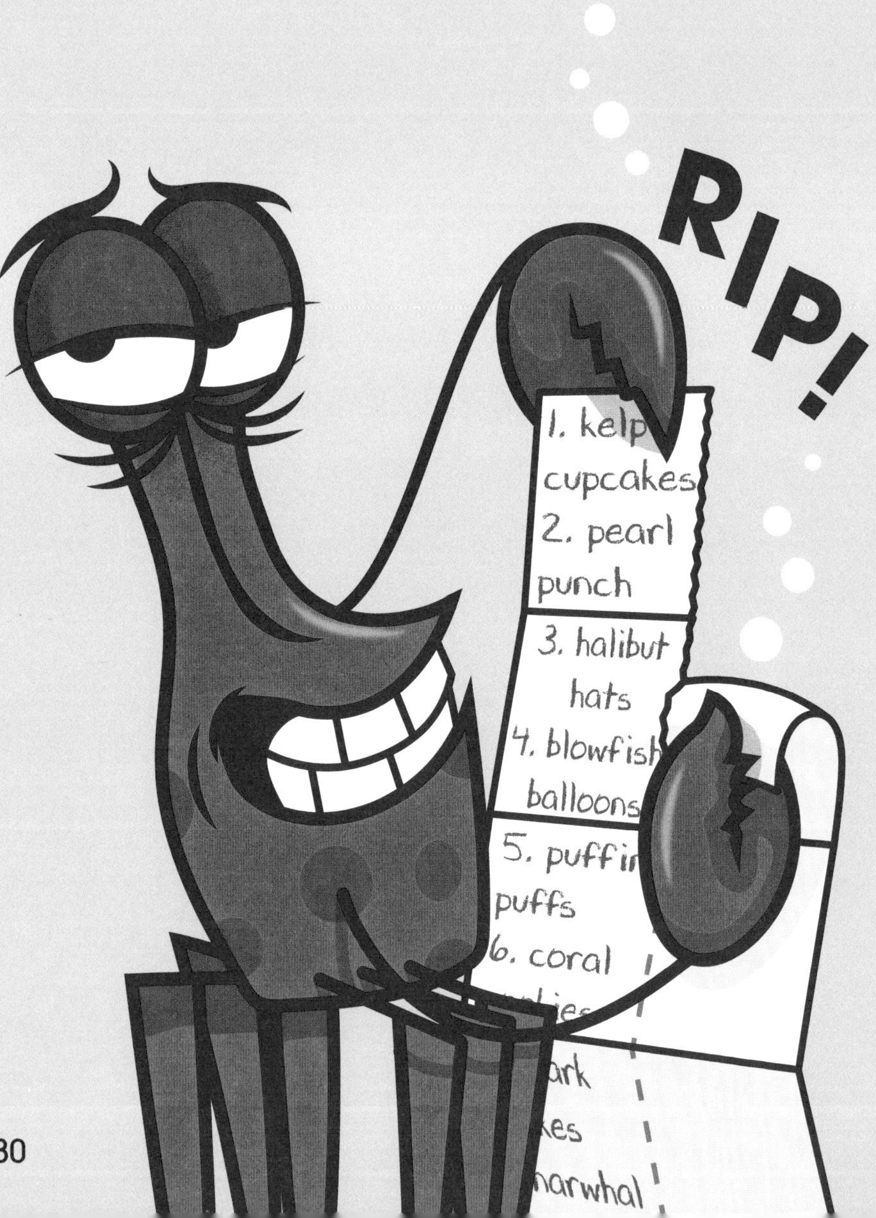
RIP!
1. kelp
cupcakes
2. pearl
punch
3. halibut
hats
4. blowfish
balloons
5. puffi
puffs
6. coral
narwhal

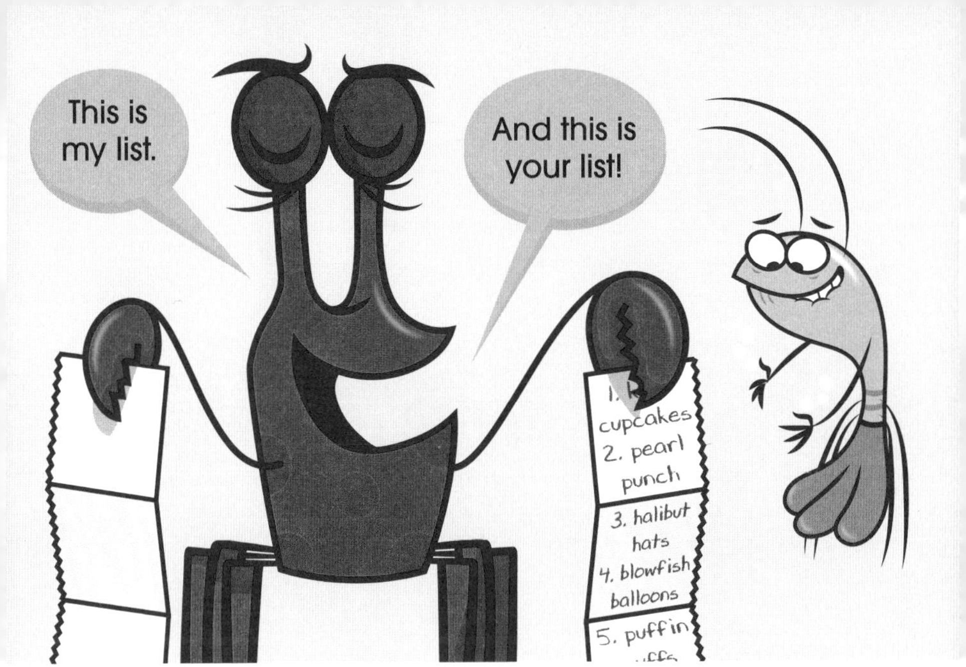
This is my list.
And this is your list!
cupcakes
2. pearl punch
3. halibut hats
4. blowfish balloons
5. puffin

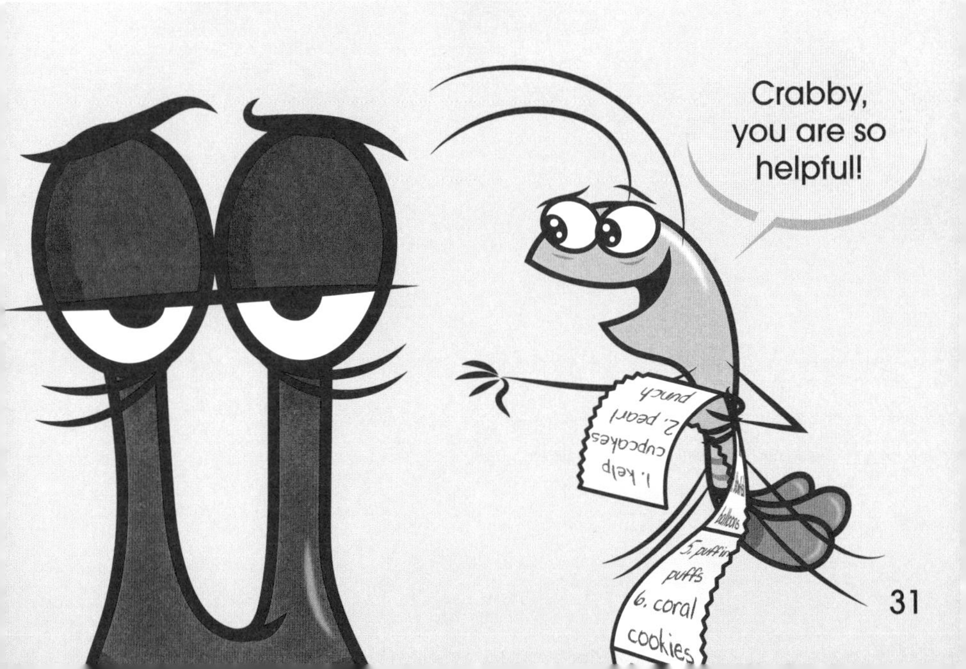
Crabby, you are so helpful!
1. kelp cupcakes
2. pearl punch
balloons
5. puffin puffs
6. coral cookies

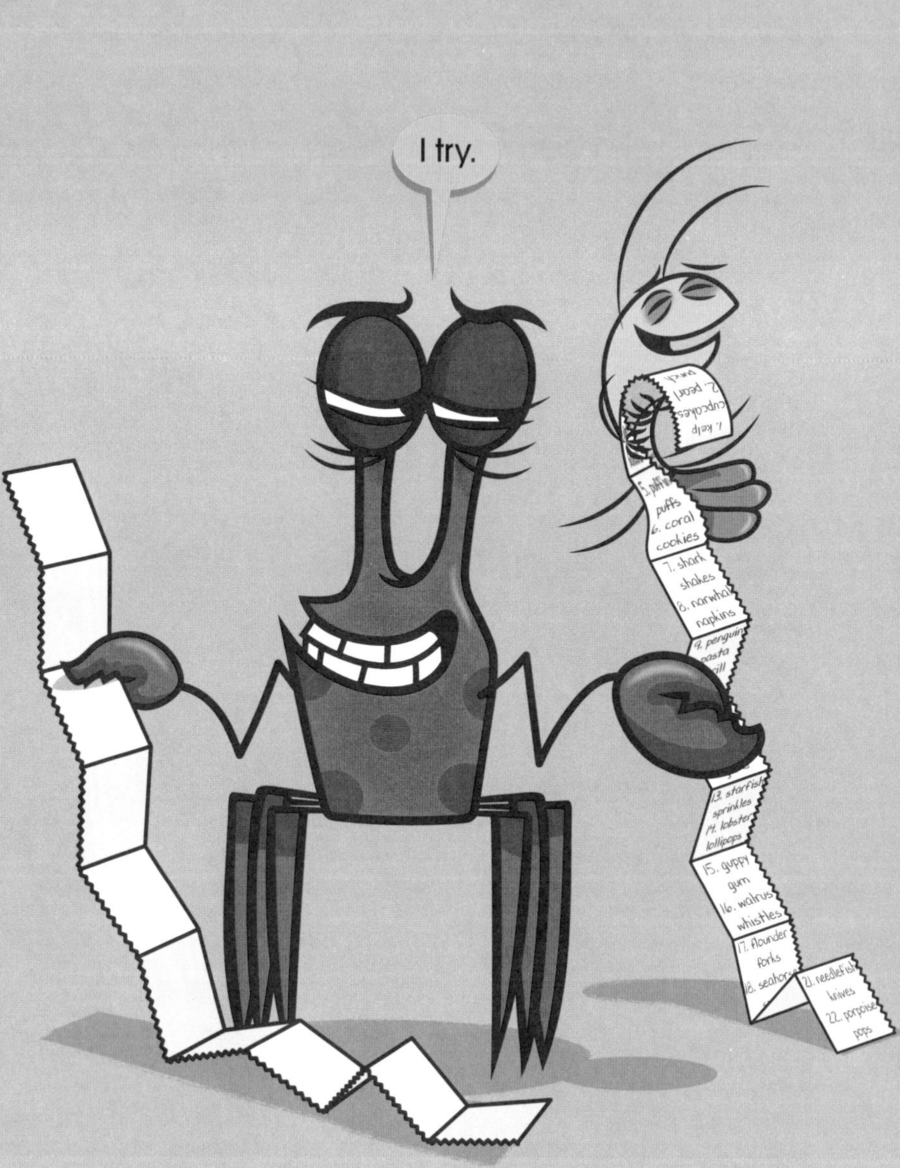
I try.
1. kelp
cupcakes
2. pearl
punch
puffs
6. coral
cookies
7. shark
shakes
napkins
9. penguin
pasta
13. starfish
sprinkles
14. lobster
lollipops
15. guppy
gum
16. walrus
whistles
17. flounder
forks
18. seahorse
21. needlefish
knives
22. porpoise
pops

THE PARTY

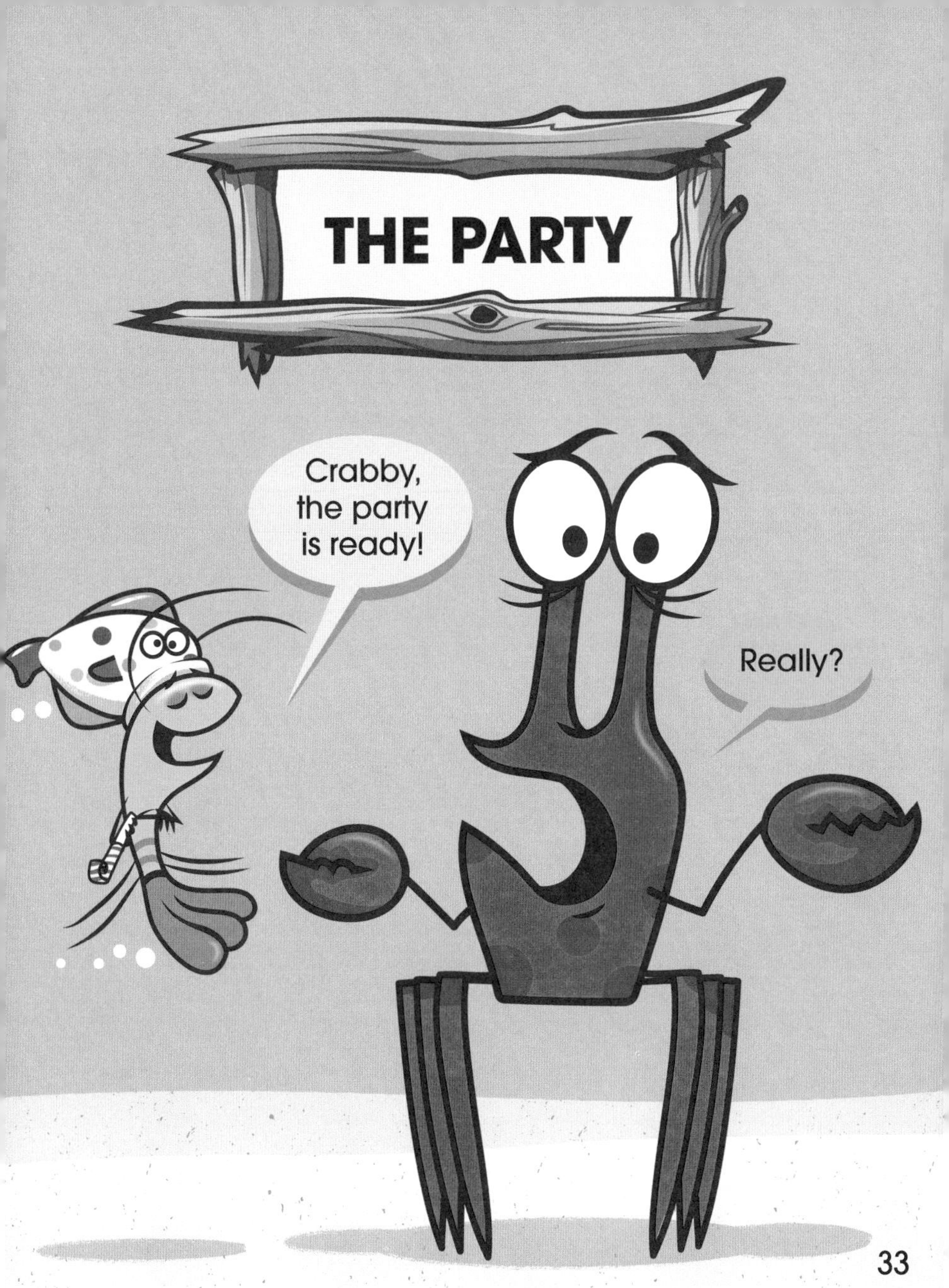
Crabby, the party is ready!
Really?

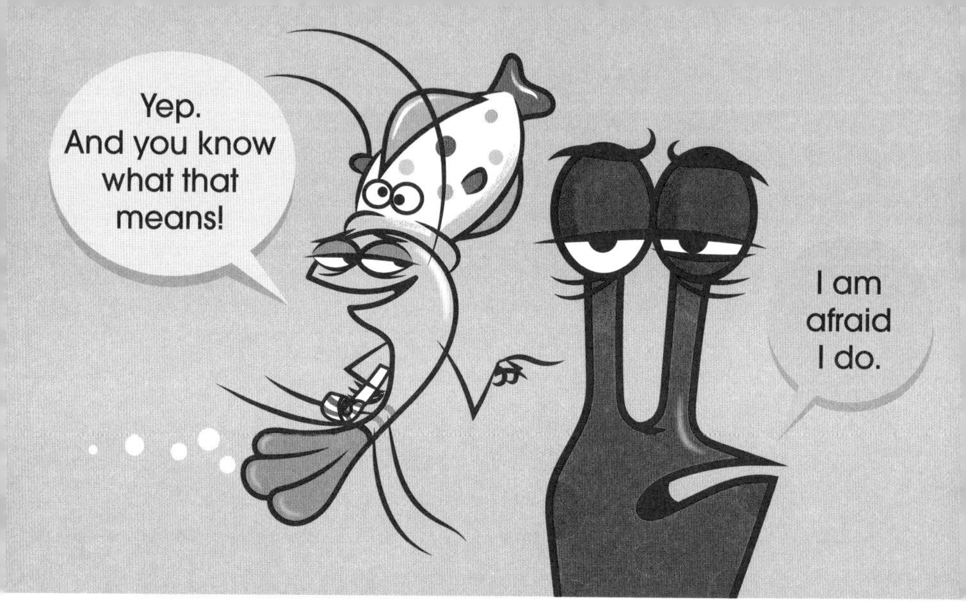
Yep. And you know what that means!
I am afraid I do.

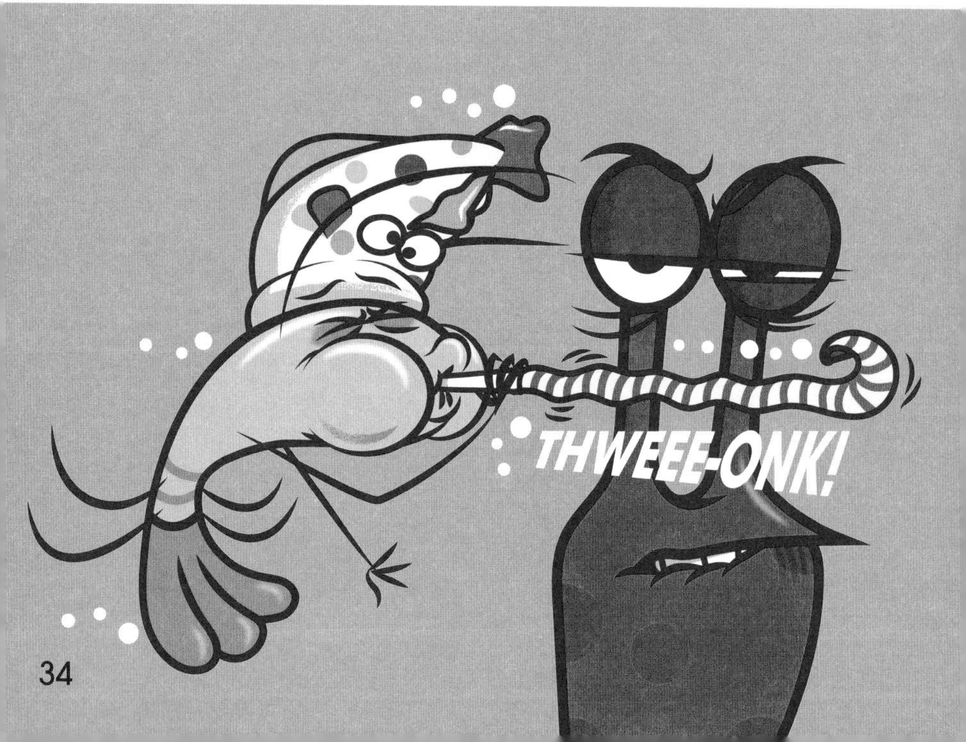
THWEEE-ONK!

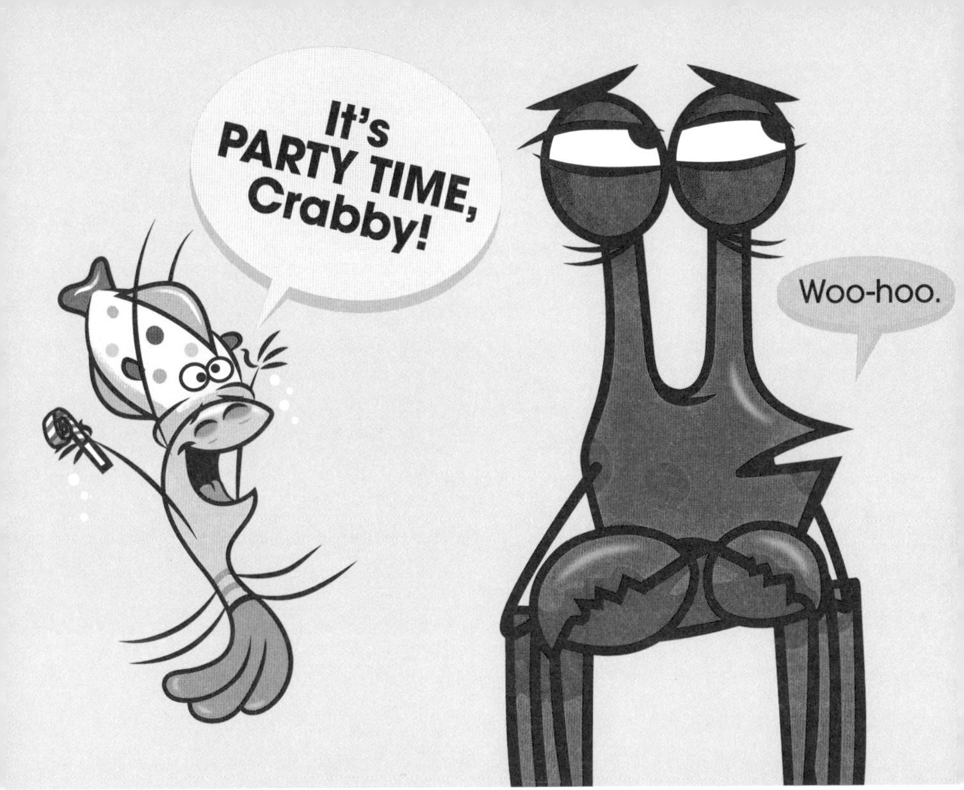
It's PARTY TIME, Crabby!
Woo-hoo.

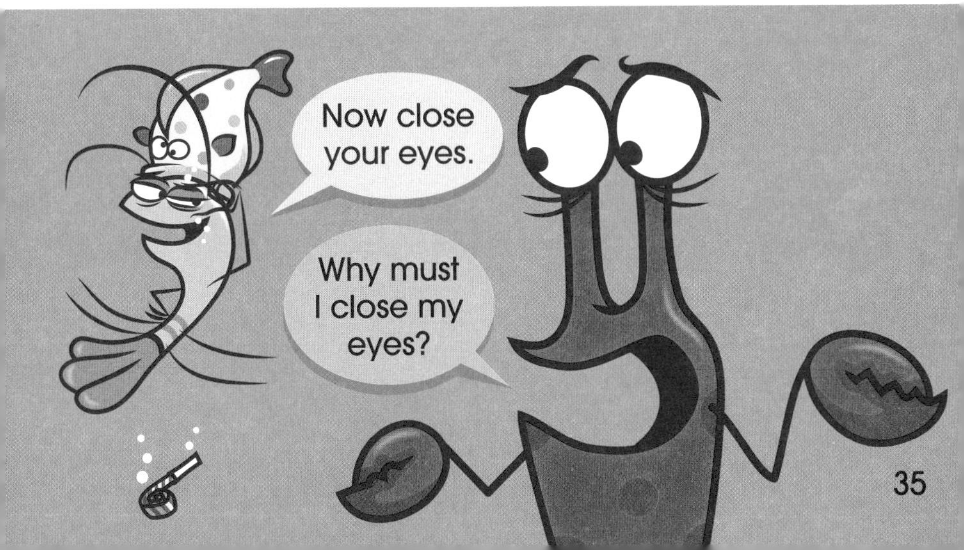
Now close your eyes.
Why must I close my eyes?

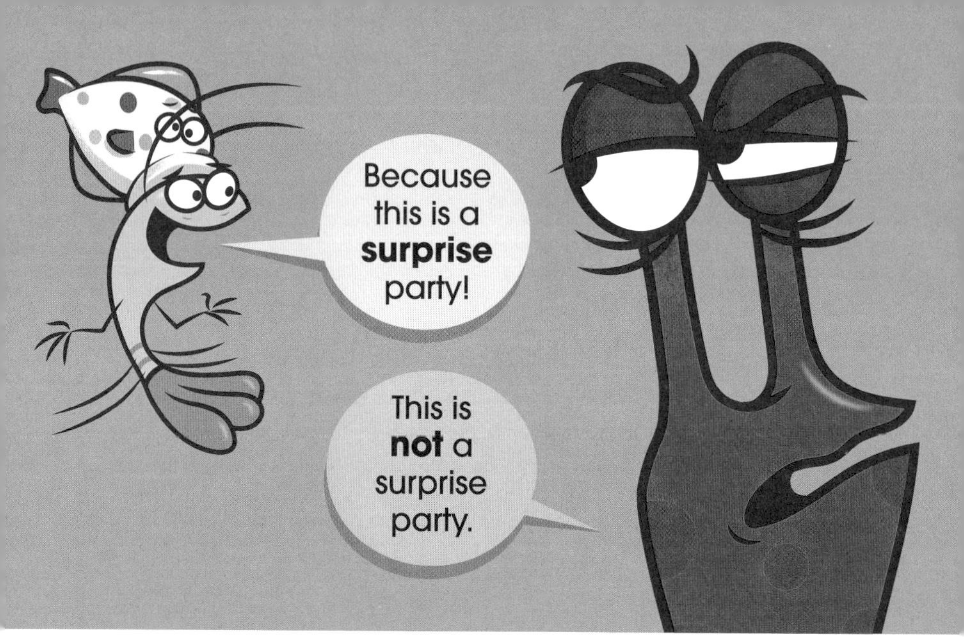
Because this is a **surprise** party!
This is **not** a surprise party.

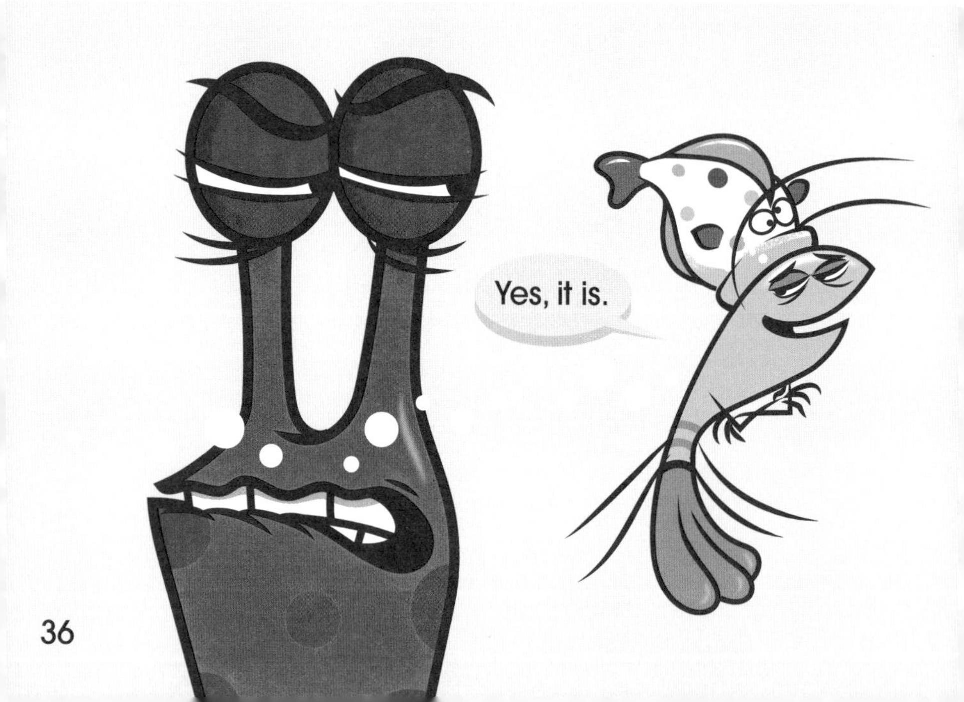
Yes, it is.

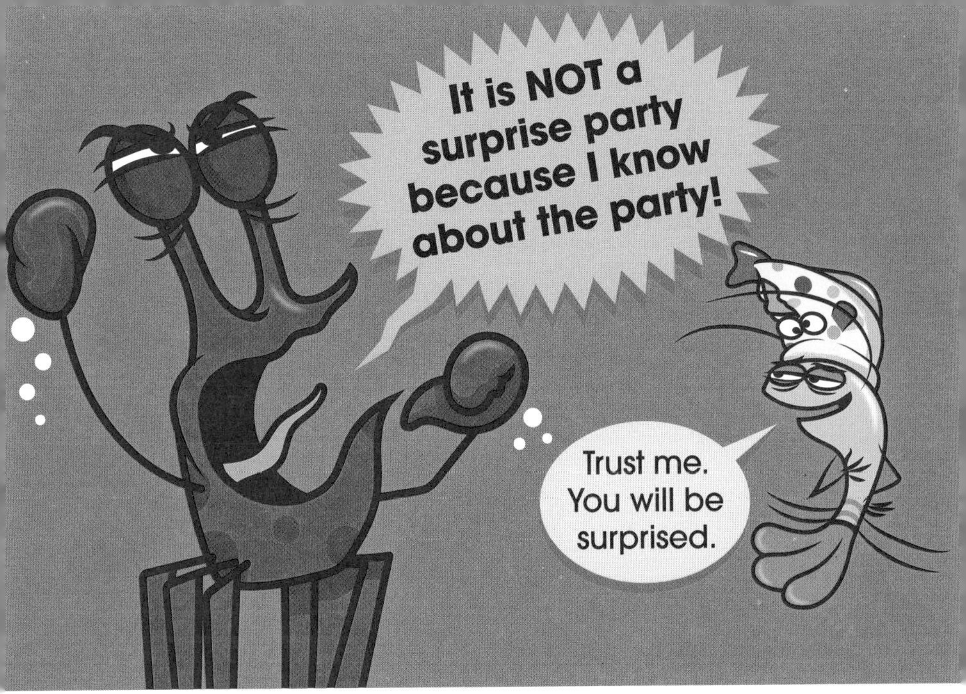
It is NOT a surprise party because I know about the party!
Trust me. You will be surprised.

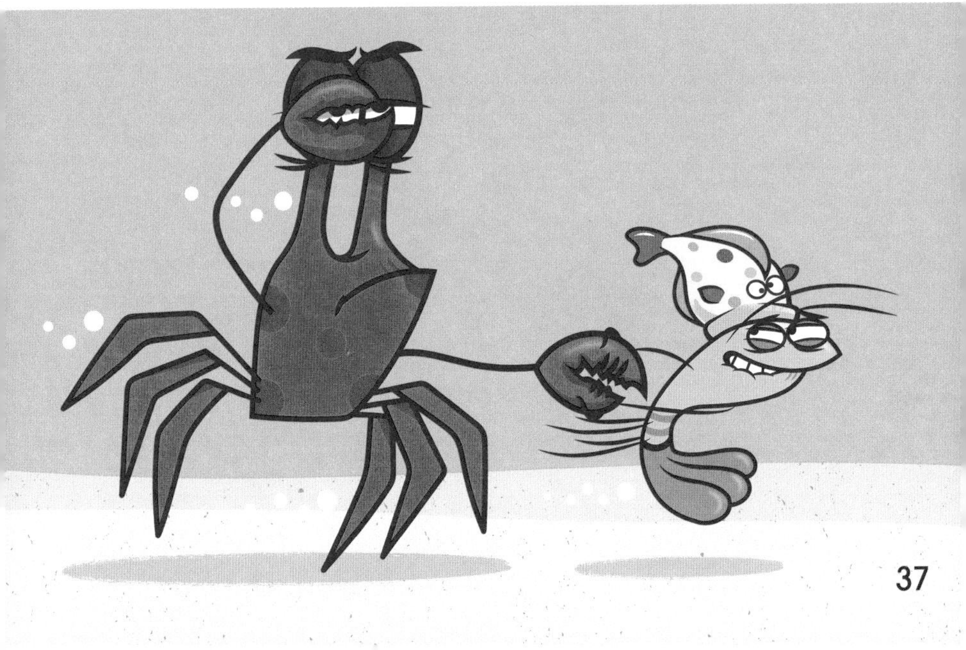

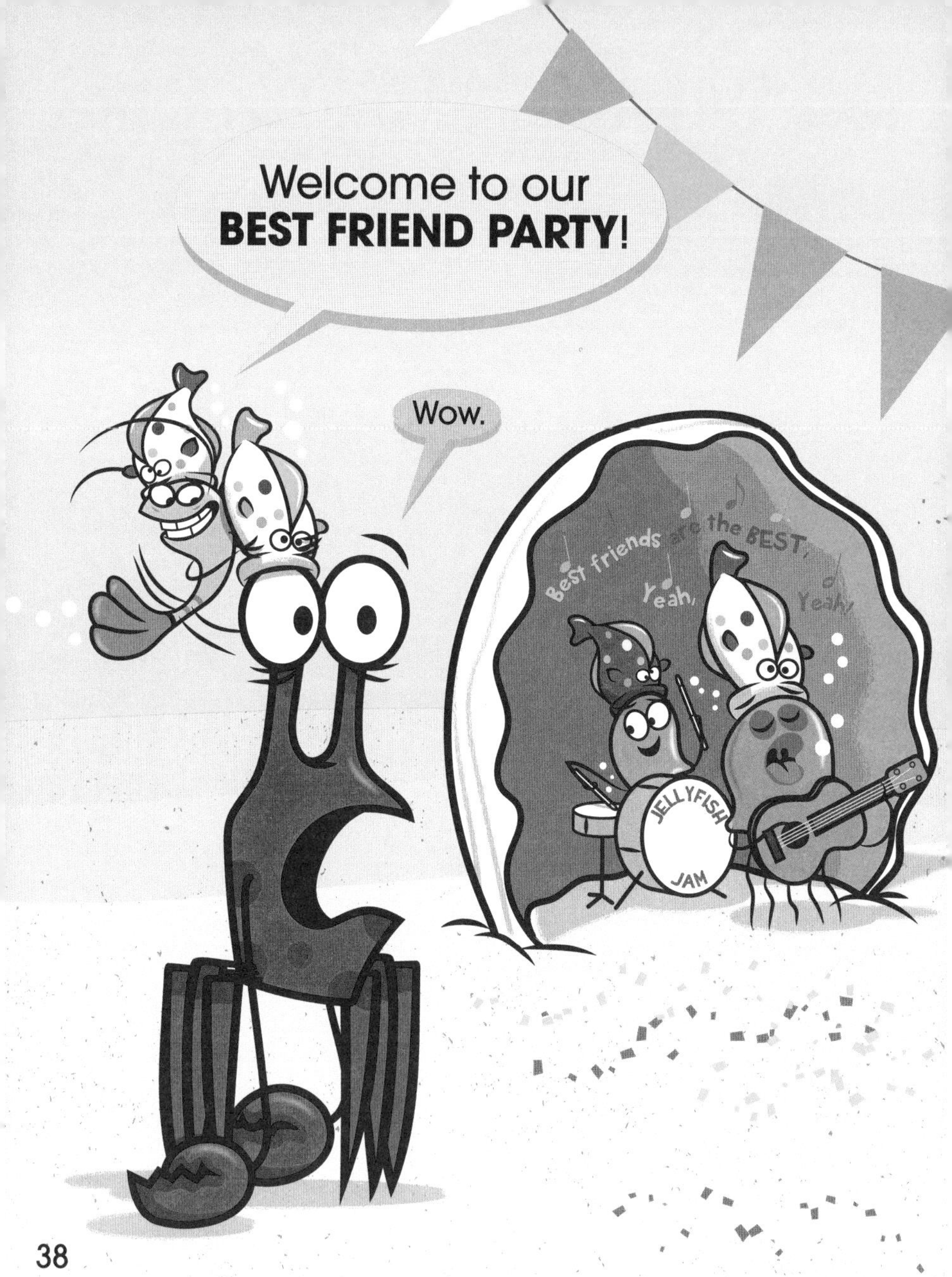
Welcome to our **BEST FRIEND PARTY**!
Wow.
Best friends are the BEST,
Yeah,
Yeah,
JELLYFISH JAM

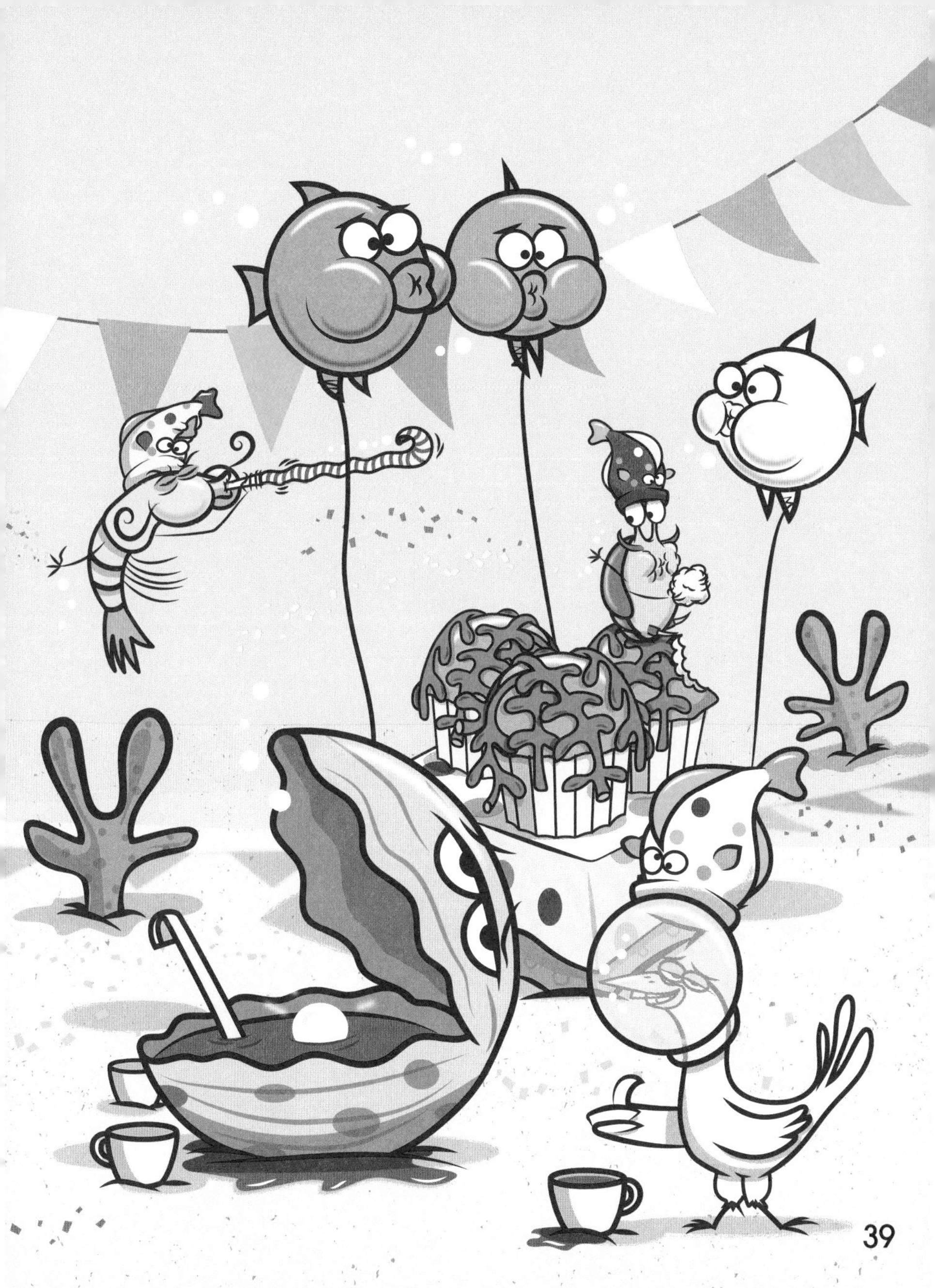

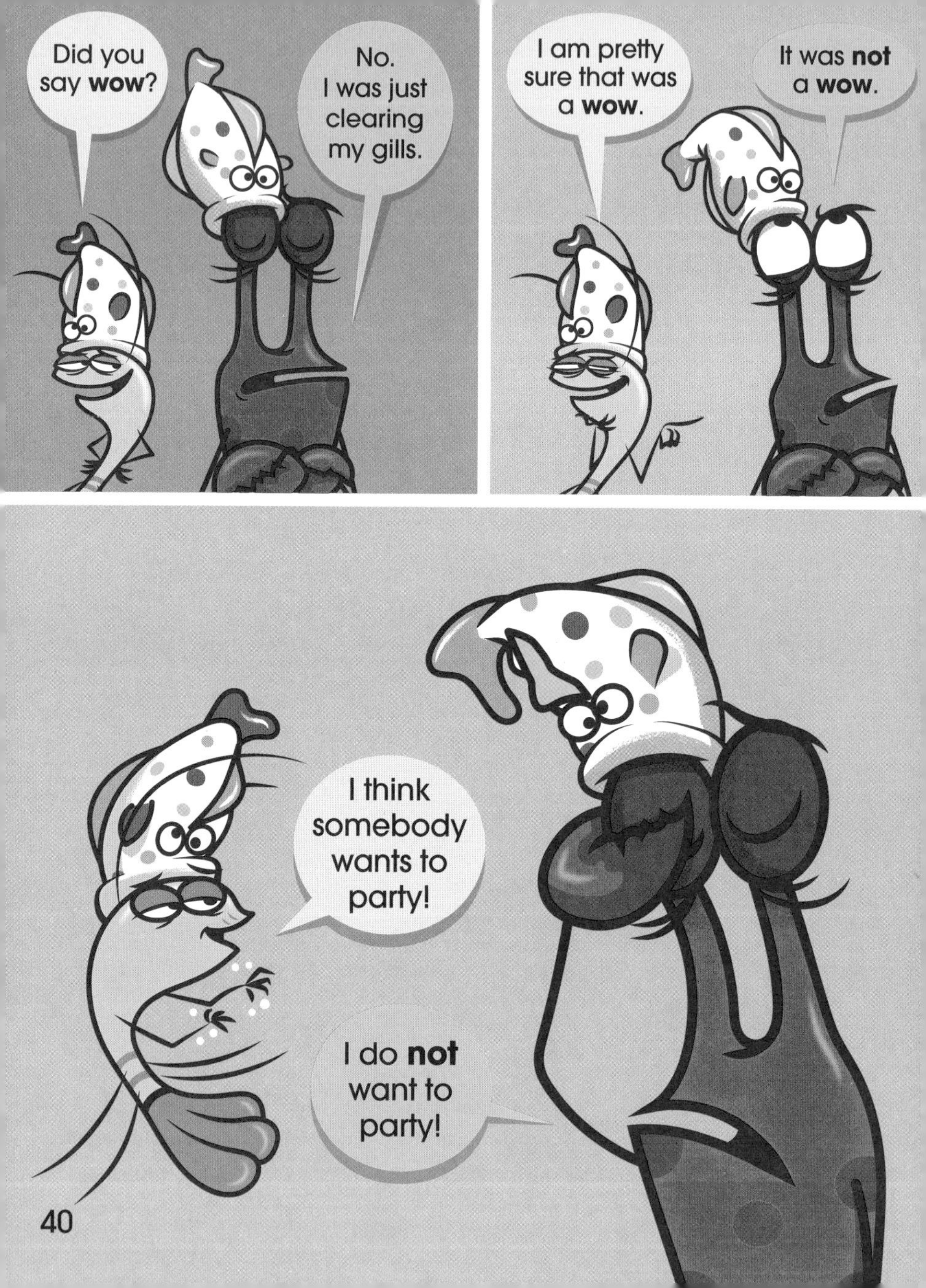
Did you say **wow**?
No. I was just clearing my gills.
I am pretty sure that was a **wow**.
It was **not** a **wow**.
I think somebody wants to party!
I do **not** want to party!

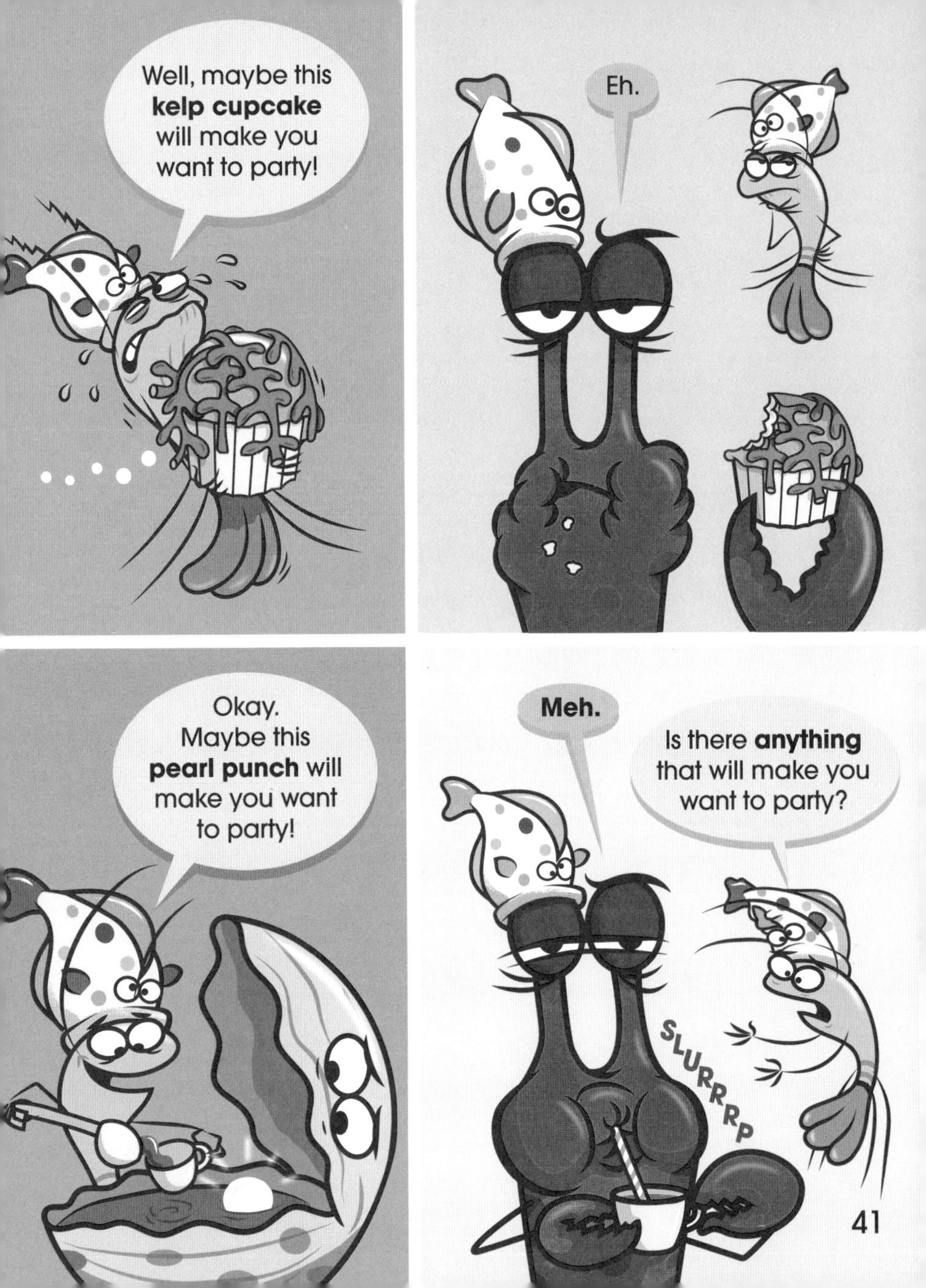

Well, maybe this **kelp cupcake** will make you want to party!
Eh.
Okay. Maybe this **pearl punch** will make you want to party!
Meh.
Is there **anything** that will make you want to party?
SLURRRRP

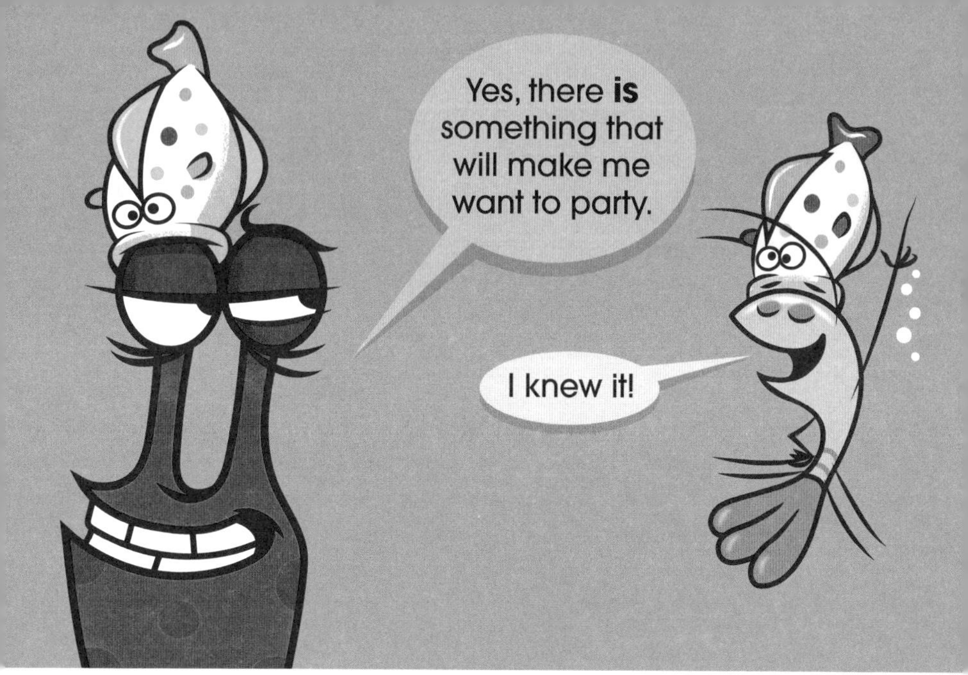
Yes, there **is** something that will make me want to party.
I knew it!

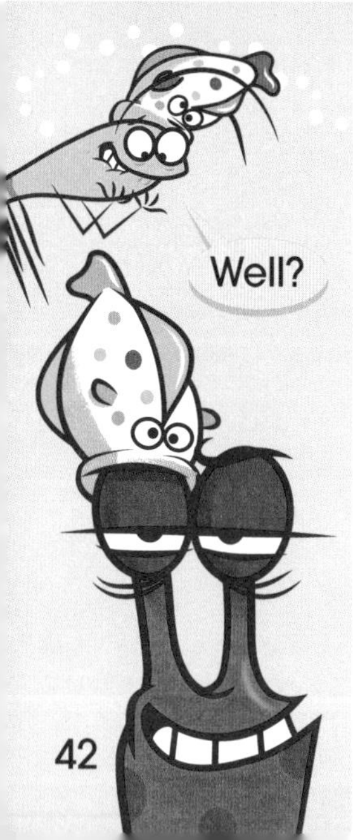
Well?

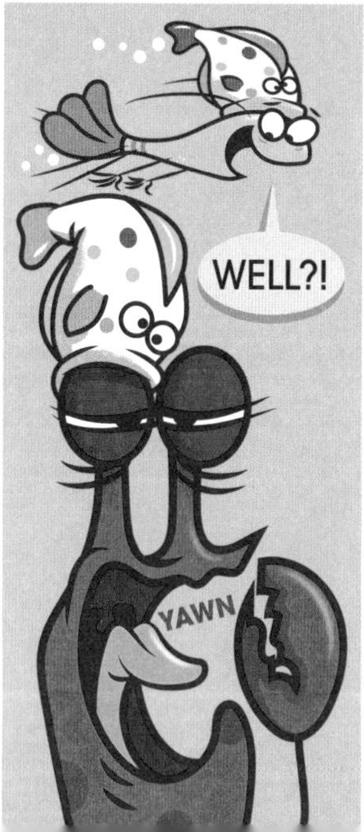
WELL?!
YAWN

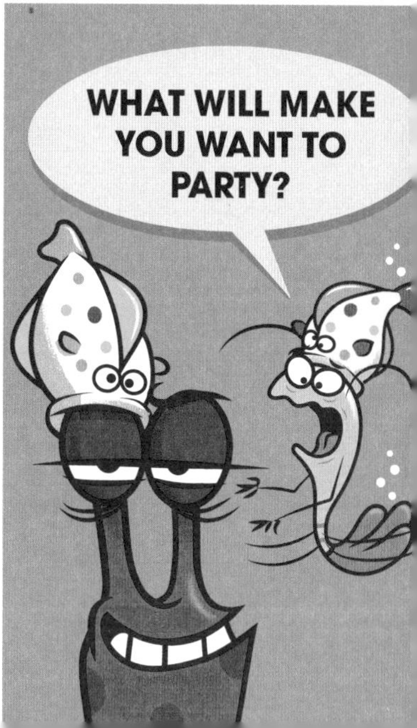
WHAT WILL MAKE YOU WANT TO PARTY?

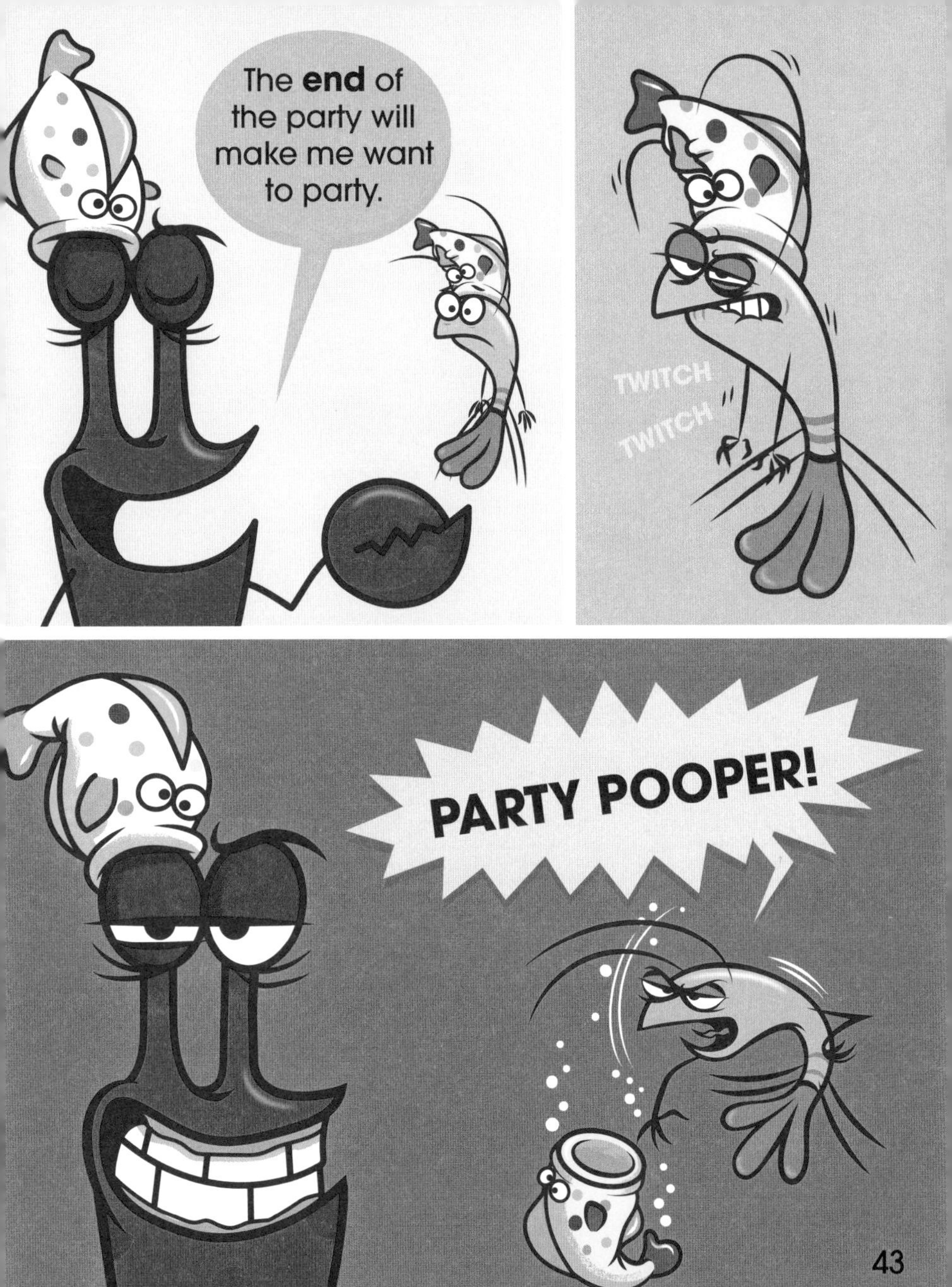
The **end** of the party will make me want to party.
TWITCH
TWITCH
PARTY POOPER!

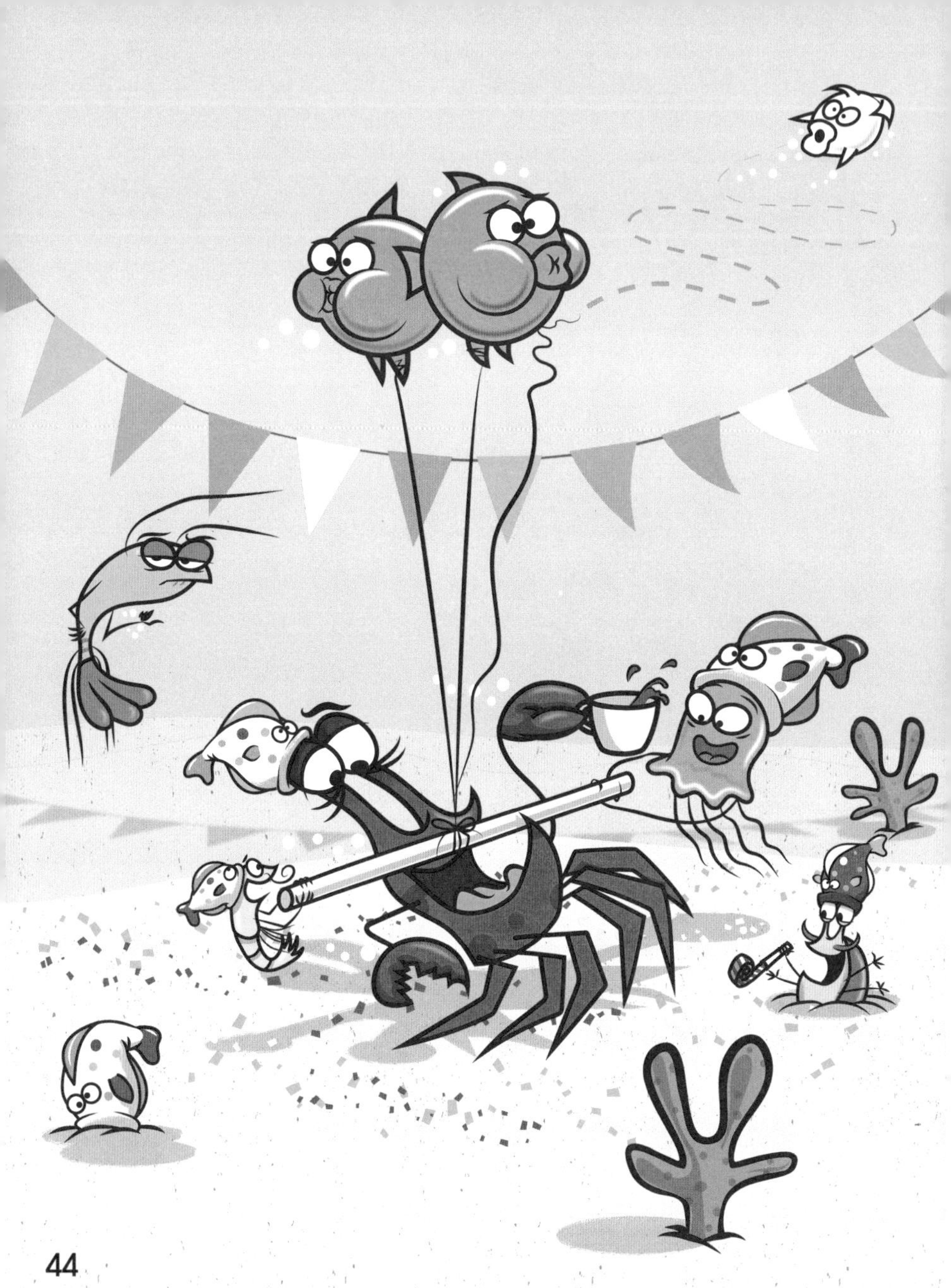

About the Author

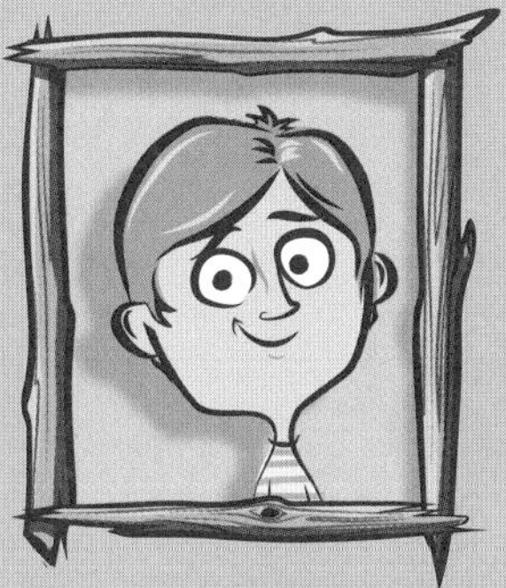

Jonathan Fenske lives in South Carolina with his family. He was born in Florida near the ocean, so he knows all about life at the beach! He thinks the best kinds of parties are small parties!

Jonathan is the author and illustrator of several children's books including **Barnacle Is Bored**, **Plankton Is Pushy** (a Junior Library Guild selection), and **After Squidnight**. His early reader **A Pig, a Fox, and a Box** was a Theodor Seuss Geisel Honor Book.

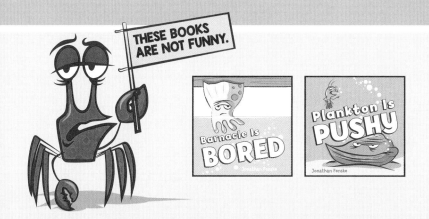

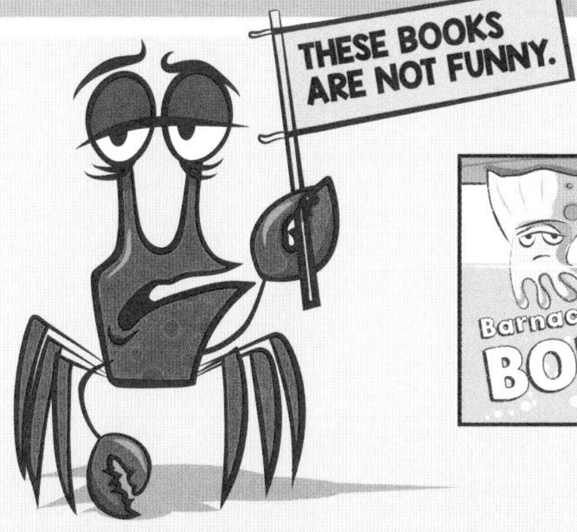
THESE BOOKS ARE NOT FUNNY.

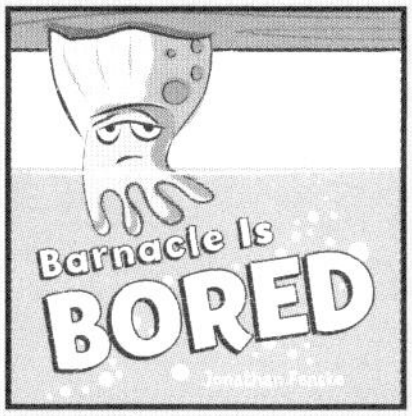
Barnacle Is
BORED
Jonathan Fenske

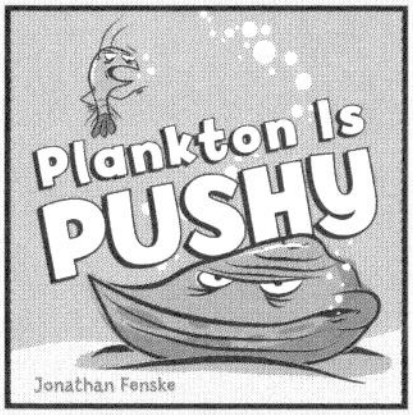
Plankton Is
PUSHY
Jonathan Fenske

YOU CAN DRAW JELLYFISH!

Wiggle. Jiggle. Squiggle!

1. Draw a curved line.

2. Use a squiggly line to connect each end.

3. Draw two eyes.

4. Draw eyebrows and a mouth.

5. Add the tentacles.

6. Color in your drawing! Don't forget the bubbles!

WHAT'S YOUR STORY?

Plankton and Crabby are having a party!
You are invited! What games will you play?
What is your favorite party food?
Write and draw your story!